D1520001

Taste the Heat

a Love and Games novel

Rachel Harris

Entangled Publishing, LLC
2614 South Timberline Road
Suite 109
Fort Collins, CO 80525
Visit our website at www.entangledpublishing.com.

Bliss is an imprint of Entangled Publishing, LLC. For more information on our titles, visit www.entangledpublishing.com.

Edited by Stacy Abrams
Cover design by Jessica Cantor

Ebook ISBN   978-1-62266-094-0
Print ISBN   978-1-49097-755-3

Manufactured in the United States of America

First Edition July 2013

The author acknowledges the copyrighted or trademarked status and trademark owners of the following wordmarks mentioned in this work of fiction: Styrofoam, Barbie, *Chopped*, *Clueless*, Chevy, Beetle, Altima, Harley-Davidson, Nancy Drew, Pottery Barn, Pepto-Bismol, Coke, Jim Beam, Jack Daniel's, Old Granddad, *American Idol*, Google, Food Network, Hershey's, Kit-Kat, Midol, Kotex, iPad, NSYNC, "You Never Even Called Me By My Name," *People*, Chanel No. 5, *Iron Chef*, *Everybody Loves Raymond*, Girl Scouts, Life Saver, iPod, *Talladega Nights*, Diet Mountain Dew, Victoria's Secret, "Fake I.D.," *Footloose*, "Country Girl," Kleenex, *The Tonight Show*, Hallmark, *Ellen*, McDonald's, Big Mac, *The Wizard of Oz*.

*To my husband, Gregg, who inspires every love story I write,
and to the city and people of the Greater New Orleans area
who have inspired not only these pages, but my entire life.*

Chapter One

When the bright red and white *Taste the Heat* banner fluttered in an abrupt and unseasonable gust of wind, then collapsed onto her head in an undignified heap, Colby Robicheaux figured it had to be an omen. Of what, she didn't really know. But considering the subject matter of both the banner *and* the multi-colored sign she had tripped over on her way up from the parking lot, she had a hunch it was a cosmic premonition of something.

"Lady Irony, you have a wicked, wicked sense of humor," she muttered, plucking the banner for the St. Tammany Parish Firefighters' Cajun Cook-off from her head. She glanced back at the aforementioned sign she'd tripped over, now standing askew in its staked position in the ground. It boasted the event's connection to the world famous New Orleans Jazz and Heritage Festival beginning the following week.

Food, music, and heritage—the trifecta so many people born and raised near New Orleans held dear. And the very things Colby had fled from twelve years ago. Lifting her eyes into the late May sun, she squinted and said, "Well played, Big Guy. Well played."

A passing snort from an event-goer made her wince. *Right.* So maybe talking to herself in public wasn't the best approach for her to prove that their family restaurant, Robicheaux's, was still in capable, non-crazy hands.

Forcing a casual, *sane* smile onto her face, she set the offending banner on the ground near the entrance of LeBeaux State Park and willed her feet to step through the gate. They refused to budge. Families and couples strolled past on their way inside, deep in conversation, hands waving dramatically as their thick accents proclaimed *dawlin'* and *yea, you right.* Others broke out in spontaneous, carefree dance to the lively Zydeco tune carried on the wind.

A memory of a similar beat hit Colby with the power of a hurricane-force wind. Suddenly she was no longer outside the park but back in her childhood kitchen, stirring a pot of gumbo as her parents danced around the butcher-block island. Her father twirled her mother in a multi-step move, and Mom's infectious laughter echoed off the oak cabinets.

Not now, please not now.

Coming home was always a tug and pull—warm memories warring with apprehension. Since she left her Las Vegas restaurant three weeks ago, Colby had yet to venture anywhere outside their small suburban town of Magnolia Springs, population 1,100. She hadn't even seen anyone beyond the restaurant staff and her siblings. In hindsight, taking a few baby steps would've been a much smarter move.

Colby gave herself a mental shake and firmly placed the ghosts of her past in the locked trunk of her memory. Back where they belonged. She straightened her shoulders, smoothed her clammy hands along the sides of her crisp linen pants, and told herself she could do this. She *owned* this.

She took a deep breath, then another for good measure, and lifted her head and marched herself through the wooded arch. Immediately, the sights, sounds, and smells of her childhood engulfed her. A large stage dominated one half of the open field with the promised Zydeco band. A woman in a brightly checkered dress sawed an accordion in and out, and a young man in crawfish-patterned suspenders sat near the edge playing a washboard. To the side, a mile-long line stretched before a photo booth with an old pirogue, crab net, and fake alligator set in front of a backdrop of the swamp. And surrounding her, encompassing the rest of the large field in a wide semi-circle, were countless booths filled with fragrant food, each representing a different St. Tammany parish firehouse.

Reading the menus posted beside the closest ones, it appeared as though they all sold jambalaya and gumbo by the Styrofoam bowlful, along with each fire station's own unique Taste the Heat twist, such as *fiery* fried jalapeno peppers, habanero nachos, and at least a dozen different forms of chili, each declaring their own to be the parish's absolute best.

The punch of spicy cayenne and fried okra assaulted Colby's senses, and the fresh onslaught was simply too much. She clamped her stinging eyes shut. She couldn't tell if the turbulent sensations rolling through her stomach were from anxiety, regret, or extreme nausea—but there was a very good chance she was about to be sick.

Oh, please God, don't let me puke in public.

She could just hear the news report now. *Big city chef returns home and tosses her cookies at local heroes' feet. Full report at ten.*

She bet that would get customers filling their tables.

"Colby Robicheaux?"

At the soft inquiry, Colby's eyes snapped open. "Ah, yes?"

The older woman standing in front of her nodded, causing her thick bob of salt-and-pepper hair to swing around her shoulders. "Thought so," she said, offering her hand in greeting. "I'm Mary Lemoine, co-organizer of today's event."

"Oh, yes. Pleased to meet you, Ms. Lemoine." She took the woman's cool hand in her own, grateful for the diversion from the emotional roller coaster, and discreetly compared her pressed linen suit with Mary's dark jeans and event T-shirt combo. She was starting to get the impression she was a tad overdressed. "Was it my Yankee attire that gave me away?"

Mary laughed, a free and open sound that instantly put her at ease. "Not at all. When your brother said you'd be stepping in as judge, I looked you up on the Internet," she confided. "Quite the impressive resume you have there. But I'd have recognized you even if I hadn't seen your picture on that fancy restaurant website of yours. You're just the spitting image of your daddy, aren't ya?"

A vision of a man beaming with pride as she created recipes beside him, while other girls her age were off playing with Barbies, flashed in her mind. It used to be that hearing people say that very thing delighted Colby like nothing else.

But those days came to an abrupt end twelve years ago.

"Here, let me show you to the judge's table." Mary gave her a sympathetic smile and motioned toward the open field, and Colby fell in step beside her. As they walked, she willed away the hurt and anger roiling inside. She knew Mary meant well, but she probably assumed Colby was upset over her father's recent passing and had no idea the real reason Colby was upset. No one did, not even her own siblings. And Colby intended to keep it that way.

As they cut a path through the sizable turnout, Mary filled her in on the details of the new venture. Colby had to admit she was impressed. All the proceeds from today's ticket and food sales went toward the St. Tammany Parish Adopt-a-Family program, an initiative co-sponsored by the local fire stations that helped people in need of clothing and basic necessities.

To help raise the needed money, event organizers had pulled out all the stops. A slew of bands were scheduled to entertain the crowd. There was face painting, a bounce house, a huge inflatable slide, and what appeared to be a wildly popular Dunk-a-Fireman booth. But the true highlight of the day, the reason she was there, was the Taste the Heat cook-off featuring three of the area's self-declared best culinary captains.

Colby listened to Mary go on about all the wonderful things the firefighters were doing for the local community, and found herself looking forward to the dishes the captains had created. Not so much tasting them, but rewarding them for their efforts. Moreover, she was thrilled to discover the painful thoughts of her past diminishing as the minutes ticked by.

Hell, she even caught herself nodding her head in time with the band's familiar beat.

Maybe today wouldn't suck so badly after all. And if today went well, then maybe everything would go well. Maybe it would be sooner, rather than later, that she'd get the family restaurant running smoothly, her siblings on solid footing, and herself back to her own life in Vegas.

With the table in view, Mary left to attend to a last-minute microphone issue and Colby made her way solo across the uneven ground. Watching her step, and not the path ahead of her, she was jolted when a preteen ball of hair plowed into her.

"Whoa, you okay there?" she asked, grasping the girl by the shoulders to steady them both.

"Yeah." The young girl flipped her blond ponytail, revealing an adorable face and bright smile. "Sorry about that.

We're playing Kiss and Catch," she explained, eyes leaving Colby's to focus on the crowd around them. "Well, the girls are playing Kiss and Catch. The boys are just running."

Colby laughed aloud. Some things never changed. When *she* was a preteen, the kissing variation of tag was more popular with the girls, too. A wide smile broke across her face as she remembered chasing her brother's best friend Jason across this very park during a particular crawfish festival. And the one time he let her catch him.

The young girl spied and then took off toward a young boy with marked intensity, tossing a smile over her shoulder. Taking her seat behind the judge's table, Colby watched the next generation of crushes, her smile growing wistful at the boy's halfhearted attempts at escape. Perhaps for the young girl, her crush wouldn't be as unrequited as Colby's had been.

• • •

Good food and even better people. Those were only two of the reasons Captain Jason Landry loved living in New Orleans, but they happened to be his favorite. And on days like today when the hellish humidity wasn't killing you, the beer was flowing and plentiful, and the sound of music and laughter surrounded him, he couldn't think of any place else he'd rather live.

"Now see, *that's* a woman for you."

He screwed the cap back on his half-empty water bottle and shook his head with a grin. So far, in just the few short hours they'd been at Taste the Heat today, his fellow captain Gavin Morris had made similar comments about at least a dozen different women—although he had to admit, the man did have impeccable taste.

Once upon a time, Jason had been right in the thick of

it with him. Carving his way through the dating scene and leaving a trail of satisfied women in his wake. But those days were long gone. Lately, any free time he had that wasn't spent working at the station or teaching classes at the gym he owned was filled with reading books about prepubescent hormones, shaving legs, and PMS. Not that he was complaining. Not really. He loved Emma, and he wouldn't trade the experience of raising his daughter for anything in the world. But being a single dad didn't exactly leave a lot of time for enjoying beautiful women.

And that was a damn shame.

On stage, the band ended their set and Mary Lemoine grabbed the microphone to announce that the cook-off would begin in a few short minutes. Good thing, too, because the warming trays they'd set up to keep their dishes hot weren't doing that great of a job.

"Yeah, she's super fine," Gavin said, still eyeing the woman in question.

The hungry crowd surged toward their end of the open field and Jason leaned forward to give his prize-winning crawfish étouffée a stir. "Oh yeah? And what's so special about this one?"

Gavin elbowed him in the side. "Why don't you take a look for yourself."

Jason re-covered the pot and glanced in the direction his friend lifted his chin toward. It took a moment for the crowd to settle and his view of Gavin's future conquest to clear, but when it did, only two words came to mind. "Hot damn."

Gavin chuckled under his breath. "My thoughts exactly." He rested his hip against the table and said, "And I've got just what she's looking for."

Jason chuckled. "She's way out of your league."

Looking back at the brunette stunner, Jason admitted she

was out of his league, too. The woman was five-alarm gorgeous. Her long dark hair hung loose around her shoulders, and her pouty lips were lifted in a contemplative smile. She bit the edge of a polished fingernail, lost in thought, and the effect was like a punch to his gut.

When was the last time he'd had such a visceral reaction to the simple sight of a woman? His fingers actually itched with the desire to wrap her hair around his palm. He bit his lip, wondering if her mouth tasted half as good as it looked.

He'd definitely been out of the scene too long.

Jason cleared his throat. "She's sitting in the judge's seat."

"And your point is?"

"My point is that if she's turned on by food, then you're shit out of luck." Pulling his attention away from the hot judge, he shot his friend a smirk. "Because my dish is gonna kick your ass."

Gavin scoffed. "In your dreams, fire boy." He pointed at the pot before him. "It so happens that my crab bisque is known for melting the panties off women." Then he grinned and gave the judge's table a pointed look. "But today, I'll settle for it working its magic on one in particular."

Jason's eyes snapped back to the brunette. That was all the prompting his imagination needed to fire up a vision of the kind of panties the woman had on—silk black thong, if he had to guess—and all the creative ways he'd like to remove them. With his teeth.

Yep, definitely been too long.

"Captains, are you ready?"

Mary's animated inquiry burst through the portable microphone, knocking the image out of his head. He quickly shifted his attention to the crowd, skin hot, knowing his eleven-year-old daughter was somewhere watching. A familiar whistle came from the far edge of the crowd and

Jason followed the sound, smiling when he found Emma. Blond hair up in its trademark ponytail, legs folded like a pretzel in his black and gold lawn chair, she held a handmade sign declaring ÉTOUFFÉE ROCKS…AND SO DOES MY DAD. Laughing, he sent her a thumbs up.

"Our three brave captains, willing to let their culinary prowess speak for itself, come from all over St. Tammany parish," Mary told the crowd. "Captain Eric Dufrene has brought his Cajun Shrimp and Grits all the way from Mandeville."

"I'm amazed I didn't get lost," Eric joked, referring to the ten-mile drive from his station to the park. Eric accepted an apron from her hands and slipped it over his head.

"And Captain Gavin Morris has brought us Crab Bisque from Covington," Mary continued, handing Gavin a black apron. Par for the course, his friend hammed it up for the crowd, flexing his muscles and smack talking as he tied it around his waist.

Jason cracked his knuckles. During all of this, the beautiful judge's eyes had followed Mary down the row. She'd offered Eric a warm smile, and laughed when Gavin bowed his head in mock-adoration. He was next. And as juvenile as it was to admit, Jason was eager for that same attention. Would she smile at him? Lower her lashes? Run her tongue along those lips?

Mary grabbed a third apron and walked toward him. The brunette glanced at her phone. Jason ground his teeth.

"And finally, our last contestant from right here in Magnolia Springs."

At that, the woman's head snapped up. Her gaze locked on him for the first time and her eyes widened as if in re-cognition. Her lips parted.

"But don't worry, folks," Mary continued. "There are no favorites here today. Everyone enters this contest on equal footing, including Captain Jason Landry and his Crawfish Étouffée."

Emma let out another sharp whistle, and Mary thrust out the apron. As Jason took the garment from her fingers, his mind churned.

They couldn't have met before. He might not have lived like a monk in the years since his wife died, but he was sure he'd remember a woman like her. He rubbed his chin, trying to recall if Mary had mentioned the judge's name when he agreed to participate, and drew a blank. Things were crazy at the station and he was dealing with Emma's newfound obsession with boys. But why hadn't he thought to ask Mary who the judge would be?

"Here's how this is gonna work." Mary nodded at a group of volunteers waiting to the side, and they came forward. "Each of our captains made enough of his dishes for everyone to have a sample, along with the tasting plate for the judge. Our volunteers will hand you a small cup of each dish and a comment card. After you've tried them all, please rank them in order of preference. Don't worry; your vote will be completely anonymous. We will tally the results and, with the judge's selection for Best Bite, the captain with the most votes will be announced the People's Choice. Make sense?"

The crowd rumbled their assent. As the volunteers handed out small plastic containers of his étouffée, Jason began prepping his tasting plate for the mysterious brunette.

Who was she? He scooped a mound of steaming white rice on the plate. On the off chance he *had* slept with her, or had met her in some other way in the past, he didn't think he should ask for her name. Women tended to prefer you remembering that sort of thing.

Was it okay to flirt with her? The woman was beautiful; regardless of how or *if* they'd met in the past, there was nothing wrong with a little harmless flirting, was there? He dipped the ladle into his étouffée and caught her smoky gaze. *As if I could help myself anyway.*

After wiping the edges of his plate clean, and adding a slice of bread and sprig of parsley for presentation, Jason made his way toward the judge's table.

"So, Captain Landry." Was it his imagination, or did her voice lilt in amusement at his title? "Can you tell me about your dish?"

"Well, ma'am," Jason began, wincing as unfamiliar discomfort prompted his ingrained Southern manners. No sexy woman wants to be ma'amed, which she proved when her cute nose wrinkled. Forging ahead, he put his and Emma's countless *Chopped* program viewing to use and said, "Today I prepared for you Crawfish Étouffée, served over jasmine rice, with a slice of warm garlic French bread." He smiled at his aspiring chef daughter and added, "Bon appétit."

. . .

Colby turned to glance at the dozens of women hanging on Jason's every word, curious as to which one of them was the lucky recipient of his sexy smile. When they were growing up, she used to dream about him flashing it at *her* one day. But not in the friendly, *how-ya-doing-squirt,* or the *I'm-your-brother's-best-friend* way he did back then. And not even the respectful *you're-the-judge-so-I-want-to-impress-you* way he did today. But in an *I-find-you-extremely-sexy* sort of way. An *I-actually-see-you-as-a-woman* way.

An *I-wanna-get-you-naked* way.

Colby choked on the peppery bite she'd just placed in her mouth.

Where in the heck had that thought come from?

Jason sprang into action, like the knight in hero's armor he'd always been, rushing to hand her a bottle of water. Colby uncapped it and quickly downed half its contents. Sure, the man—or rather, the boy he once was—had filled the pages of her childhood diary, and not all of her whimsical fantasies had been PG-rated. But the last time she'd even come close to getting naked with a man was more than three years ago. A very _long_ three years ago.

Colby looked up into Jason's concerned brown eyes, glanced at the scar slashing his left eyebrow, and took another long gulp.

"Are you all right?" He squatted down beside her chair, the fabric of his dark blue uniform pants stretching taut over his thighs. The Louisiana heat skyrocketed.

She nodded, and with a self-deprecating laugh he asked, "Was it my cooking?"

"No, it was my fault," she answered, searching his handsome face for any sign that he knew who she was. "It just went down the wrong way."

He lifted his hand and then hesitated, hovering it in mid-air until finally placing it over hers in an obvious gesture of comfort. Colby swallowed against the energy zinging up her arm. Tall and dark with piercing eyes and an easy smile, young Jason had set more than just her heart fluttering back in the day. But the man he'd grown into was simply devastating.

Strong, work-roughened fingers encircled her slender wrist. Her eyelids flickered. This small, innocent touch was the most action she'd gotten in a while. Then the thick pad of Jason's thumb grazed across her skin moments before his nail rasped the tender flesh near her pulse. Her insides clenched. Looking up, she saw unmistakable attraction flash in his toffee-colored eyes. And then his hand was gone.

"Good," he finally said, pushing to his feet. "I'd hate to be the one responsible for poisoning the judge." He slid her one of his signature sexy, lopsided grins and headed back to his side of the table.

Colby couldn't believe it. He actually didn't recognize her. She knew it had been almost eight years since she'd last seen him at her mother's funeral, when she'd looked like the living dead, but she hadn't changed *that* much since they were kids. At least she didn't think she had.

He certainly hadn't.

Under the tailored MSFD uniform shirt, Jason's back muscles flexed as he walked away. Yeah, he was older. His shoulders were broader, his waist trimmer. His backside filled out his uniform pants in a way that had her wanting to squeeze it. But he was still Jason. She remembered when he'd gotten that slash above his eyebrow. She was there when he broke his nose in her driveway. Well, being a girl and three years younger, she had observed most of it from the window seat in her bedroom, but she was *there*.

From a few feet over, Mary discreetly cleared her throat, reminding Colby of where she was. With reluctance, she slid her eyes away from Jason's delectable ass and glanced at the large crowd seemingly hanging on their every exchanged word. It wasn't that their banter so far had been overtly flirtatious, but for some reason it *felt* like it was.

This is why I stay in the kitchen, she thought, picking up her fork and spearing a plump crawfish tail. *In public, it's only a matter of time until I make an idiot of myself...or drool all over hot firemen.*

"This is quite delicious," she told the smoldering firefighter before her, taking another small bite.

And really, objectionably she knew that it was, although that's where the real irony of today came into play. The local fare may've been a staple of her diet growing up, and as a chef,

Colby could still appreciate the cuisine's signature spicy burst of flavor, but she hadn't personally touched the stuff since she was eighteen. And nothing even remotely Cajun was on her restaurant menu back in Vegas.

It wasn't that the food wouldn't sell—she knew it would. Hell, people asked her about it whenever they heard where she was from. But Colby could never handle the sting of memories that preparing it conjured. The rush of emotion that came with the distinct aroma. Yet here she was, *temporary* acting head chef at an established Cajun restaurant in the metropolitan area she'd vowed never to return to, and judging a festival celebrating the very cuisine she'd left behind.

Her big brother *so* owed her.

But the flavors Jason created were perfectly balanced, with a nice burst of peppery goodness at the end. It brought her right back to the days in her father's kitchen, and it was obvious he had a skillful hand.

"You cooked your roux down perfectly." She licked a dollop of sauce off her top lip. "You made your own stock from the shells, didn't you?"

His intent stare, which had been glued to her mouth as she ate, lifted at her question. "Yeah, I did," he said, obviously taken aback. "That's impressive. Although, I guess it's your job to know that kind of thing, right?"

She set down her fork and wiped her mouth with a napkin. "It is, but there's also an undeniable difference between étouffée prepared with homemade stock, and étouffée without it." She smiled. "It's a whole lot quicker to leave it out, or to go with the stuff you can buy in a store. But in my experience, it's always better to take your time and do it right."

Jason's ready grin widened into a wicked smile and she could feel herself blushing at the potential double meaning of her words. It was almost surreal. She was flirting with the man who'd starred in every childhood fantasy she ever had—in public no less. And *he* was flirting right back. Had someone told her preteen or even teenage self that there would be a day Jason Landry came on to her, Colby never would've believed it. A few minutes ago, her adult self would've said it didn't matter because she'd sworn off men when she was eighteen. But the reality of it happening, even if he didn't know who she was—or maybe *because* he didn't—was just too tempting to ignore.

Any minute now, he'd figure it out. Cane had promised he'd stop by, and if seeing his best friend there didn't clue Jason in, she was sure Mary would announce her name eventually. But until then, Colby figured she might as well have a little fun...for her young self's sake, of course.

"Well done, Captain Landry," she said, instinctively lowering her voice to a more obvious coquettish tone. Inwardly, she cringed at the pathetic attempt at flirting. *It really has been too long.* Jason took a step forward and she looked up at him through her lashes, her brain apparently embracing the pathetic. "Obviously this isn't your first rodeo."

Jason's firm mouth twitched. "I know my way around a kitchen."

She had no doubt there were several rooms the man knew his way around.

Clicking the button on the top of her ballpoint pen, she bit back a smile. "I'll be sure to keep that in mind. Thank you, Captain."

Jason bowed his head and slowly backed away from the table, brown eyes never leaving hers. The giddy rush of feminine power running through her veins, along with a heady dose of sexual attraction, was unlike anything she'd felt in years. It really was too bad it would all end the moment he discovered who she was.

Reluctantly, Colby broke the toe-tingling eye contact. She jotted down a few notes about the dish, as if she'd ever forget, and Mary called Captain Morris to the table. But as much as the good-looking man tried flirting with her, and as appealing as his dish was, her gaze kept transferring back to Jason.

At the end of the competition, after all the crowd's votes had been tallied, Captain Dufrene had been announced as the People's Choice. Eric lifted his award plaque high in the air, and then everyone quieted to hear which dish would be crowned Best Bite.

As Mary accepted the slip of paper she'd written the winner's name on, Colby caught sight of her brother weaving through the crowd. Cane always did have impeccable timing.

The woman silently read the result, then smiled at the crowd. "All of our contestants today should be proud. Not only did they do a fabulous job representing their districts, and help raise money for a very important program, but their food was tasted by one of our country's leading female chefs—and a Magnolia Springs native."

The crowd murmured as Cane plopped into an empty chair beside her. "Looks like I got here just in time," he whispered, leaning close to her ear. "Who did you pick?"

Colby didn't answer. She was too busy watching Jason mentally put the puzzle pieces together. His befuddled gaze moved from her to her brother and to Mary, then back again. His eyes narrowed...and then widened. *Bingo.*

"That's right," Mary continued, as if talking directly to Colby's childhood crush. "Our own Colby Robicheaux left her fancy Vegas digs and can now be found back where she belongs. Right here, at a certain local family restaurant we all know and love."

Beside her, Cane reached out and squeezed Colby's

shoulder. Jason pressed a fisted hand to his mouth, shaking his head in apparent disbelief.

"And for today's Best Bite, Colby has chosen...drum roll, if you please." The crowd quickly granted her request and after a few moments of simulated beats, Mary proclaimed, "Magnolia Springs Captain Jason Landry and his delicious étouffée! Congratulations, Captain. Come and collect your prize!"

Chapter Two

So little Colby Robicheaux wasn't so little anymore.

That's the thought that ran through Jason's head as he accepted his plaque and thanked the crowd. He nodded in gratitude and slid his best friend a smile. Since Cane returned it, Jason assumed he must've missed seeing him hit on his little sister...but from the knowing looks their neighbors sent in his direction, Cane was the only one. And the beauty of living in a small town meant it was only a matter of time before someone filled him in.

As Jason gathered his things together, he replayed their flirtation and cringed. Why in the hell hadn't he recognized her sooner? Growing up, he'd practically been an honorary Robicheaux. He lost track of the amount of family vacations he'd tagged along on, the holidays he'd crashed, and the nights he'd spent sleeping on their couch. Colby was the kid sister who followed him around, not a woman with smoky eyes and a wicked smile that tempted him to do things he had no business thinking.

When was the last time he'd seen her? She'd come in for her father's funeral a few months ago, but the memorial had been for family only. The man hadn't wanted anything traditional, just his ashes spread at his favorite fishing spot in Lafitte, so the three siblings had done it privately. Then Colby had turned right back around for her fancy restaurant in Vegas. That would make it at least seven or eight years.

He stole a glance at the judge's table. Colby stood there with Cane, listening as Mary droned on about something or other and then led them toward the Magnolia Springs food booth. Her hair was longer, her wardrobe much better than it used to be. He grinned, remembering a few of her former fashion disasters, swinging from her obsession with the movie *Clueless* to her love affair with Kurt Cobain. And adult Colby's body…well, from the way the suit clung to her curves, she had definitely grown up from the sixteen-year-old he'd left behind when he went to college. But watching her and her brother walk side by side, the resemblance between them was obvious.

A pair of skinny arms wrapped around his waist a moment before his daughter's head plowed into his stomach. "Way to go, Dad! I knew those suckers didn't have a chance."

Jason winked at Gavin and Eric over Emma's head. "How could I lose with such an amazing sous-chef?" He placed a kiss atop her ponytail. "I believe it was your idea to add a homemade stock to the recipe."

"You can't shortcut taste," she said wisely. She stepped out of the embrace and pushed herself up onto the table. "So, was that really Uncle Cane's sister?"

Jason glanced back to where he'd last seen them at the booth and winced. Being her godfather, Cane was always referred to as Emma's uncle. But somehow hearing the term of affection now just made what he did seem worse. "Yep, that was Colby."

She squealed. "And she's *really* a big-city chef who left

her restaurant to come here?" Jason nodded again, and his aspiring-chef daughter nearly bounced off the table. "That is so cool!"

He couldn't help laughing at her enthusiasm. And she was right. Despite the stickiness of the situation, Colby coming back was very good news. Cane had been living under a mountain of stress being in charge of a thriving restaurant that no longer had a head chef. He'd gone through several failed hires since their father died two months ago, all while trying to keep the restaurant running. Having Colby back would ease the strain and, hopefully, help make Robicheaux's profitable again.

"Yeah," he said, rubbing a hand over the top of his daughter's head. "I guess that is pretty cool."

Emma batted him away with a groaned, "Dad," then squealed again when they announced her favorite group, the Joey Thomas Band, was taking the stage. Throwing her arms around his neck and giving him a peck on the cheek, she muttered another quick, "Congratulations," and then ran to the stage.

"If only they could bottle that energy," he said to himself, watching her make her way to the front. After ensuring she was safe with a group of friends and standing in plain sight, Jason turned back to the row of booths. But Cane and Colby had disappeared.

He ran a hand over his face. It was almost funny. The one woman actually to get his blood pumping again—the first in he didn't even know how long—and she ended up being completely off-limits. As far as his luck went, that seemed about right.

It wasn't *just* that she was Cane's little sister, although that did pretty much kill it right there. He could only imagine how that conversation would go. *Hey man, your sister's hot. Mind if I take her for a spin?* No. Just no.

And it wasn't *just* that Jason had been there when Colby got her first zit or that he accidently saw her naked when she was in junior high. It wasn't even that he was one of the many people she had left behind so easily all those years ago, or that he knew how much her desertion affected her family.

The biggest reason Colby was a no-go was Emma.

Jason looked back at the stage. If he'd learned anything from all his recent late-night reading, it was that his daughter needed a solid female presence in her life. Sure, his mom did an amazing job, helping as often as she could and keeping her during his twenty-four-hour shifts. But the best grandparenting in the world couldn't replace having a day-to-day woman in the house. A mother she could talk to about boys. Help her pick out a bra and makeup. And know what the hell a loofah was used for. Jason had been good with little girl Emma. He could handle cuts and scrapes and training wheels. But an Emma on the verge of womanhood? A teenager with questions about hormones and boys and *sex*? That mess scared the crap out of him.

When Ashleigh died four years ago, getting remarried was the last thing on Jason's mind. Falling in love again *still* was. His high school sweetheart had been the undisputed love of his life and no woman could ever replace her. But having a partner, a friend, someone to share his day with and be a role model for Emma wouldn't be so bad.

The starry-eyed girl he'd grown up with, though, would never settle for something like that. She would want more, and *deserved* more, than the loveless, convenient-marriage life he was offering. Even *if* her big brother didn't kick the shit out of him for thinking it—which he would, so the point was moot anyway. Jason couldn't waste his time on flirtation and dating, and he wasn't willing to risk his heart again, which left him and his best friend's sister at an impasse.

No, regardless of how hot Colby was—and there was no doubt about it, the woman was smoking—she was definitely off-limits.

Chapter Three

Jason shook his head in disgust as he drove down Main Street. Tall pines and moss-draped oaks stood on either side of the winding state highway that passed through Magnolia Springs. Normally, after a long or stressful day, this stretch of road chilled Jason out. Helped him think clearly and gain perspective. But today, he just felt restless. His knee bounced up and hit the console.

He told himself he was going to see Cane. Life had been so hectic the past few months that other than discussing skills from the tactical ninjitsu classes Jason taught twice a week, they'd barely managed to issue a passing hello. Jason couldn't remember the last time he went by Cane's work for a simple visit. So *that* was why he was headed there now. To catch up, see what was new in his best friend's world. It had nothing to do with a certain hot brunette now manning the kitchen.

And if anyone believed *that*, Jason had a mountain chalet down the road to sell him.

Reaching over, he blasted the air-conditioning in his trusty Chevy, fighting against the already brutal heat. He turned up the radio to drone out his thoughts and tapped his hand on the steering wheel, singing along to Tim McGraw. The song was about a dad and his little girl, and the lyrics had him thinking back to his breakfast with Emma. God, she was growing up so fast. The first year after his wife died, life had slowed to the pace of Louisiana politics. But lately it was as if things were going at warp speed, determined to make up for lost time. When she had come to the table that morning, he'd had to bite his tongue at the swipe of hooker-red lipstick on his sweet daughter's lips. But when he caught Emma doodling a heart around a boy's name, he'd lost it.

Not one of his finer moments for sure, but when did his tree-climbing daughter start caring about things like makeup? And who the hell was this Brad kid? Did he know that her father was trained in hand-to-hand combat? Jason made a mental note-to-self to let the kid in on that not so little secret just in case.

This was why he was hitting the pavement even though it was his day off. If he hung out at home, all he'd accomplish would be more worrying. He was no good without a plan. He needed to be productive. Useful. Busy. That's why he'd opened up the gym. With his schedule at the department of twenty-four hours on, forty-eight off, he needed something else to occupy his time. Plus, the house was too quiet during the day without Emma's endless chatter.

But he didn't have to be at the gym until six, a drawback of hiring such efficient managers and support staff. So he'd headed to the firehouse, knowing that if he weren't there to cook lunch the men would just order pizza. He'd slid the leftover crawfish étouffée into the well-stocked refrigerator, hung his winning plaque on the wall, and accepted his share of ribbing and congratulations from his co-workers. Then, he'd hopped back in the truck and steered it toward Robicheaux's. Where he had known he'd end up all along.

"I'm an idiot."

Colby was the last thing he should be thinking about right now. She was not the woman he needed. She'd want more than he could give, her brother would kill him for even thinking it, and he *should* think of her like a sister. But none of that had stopped him from thinking about her. Maybe seeing her again at Robicheaux's, talking with her out in the open now that he knew who she was, would ease his curiosity.

Throwing his truck into park, Jason took in the family restaurant located in the heart of the town. It was a renovated Southern home on the north shore of Lake Pontchartrain. Clean white paint and a wrap-around porch surrounded by crepe myrtles and azaleas welcomed all, but the real draw was the large back porch overlooking the water.

Over the years, it had evolved into a retreat for the community, a place where locals gathered to uncork a bottle of wine, listen to live music, and watch the sun set over the lake. Old Mr. Robicheaux would often hang out there with his customers, laughing and talking until closing time…and often past that. That was why the man's heart attack had rocked their small community so much. Robicheaux's wasn't just a place to eat. It was where friends, family, and an occasional straggler would get together to share life.

Jason looked around the gravel lot. Other than Sherry's magenta-colored Bug and an ancient-looking, silver Altima, the place was a ghost town. Not unusual for two thirty in the afternoon on a Monday, but it did make his appearance all the more obvious. He also noticed the absence of a certain Harley. Though that didn't stop him from marching up to the beveled glass door and tugging it open.

A series of bells *ding*ed overhead. From the back of the restaurant, the youngest Robicheaux came flying, menus in hand, long stripes of purple tresses streaming behind her.

"Oh," she said, halting abruptly when she saw who was there. "It's only you."

Jason laughed. "Gee, Sher, it's good to see you, too."

She smiled and the restlessness in him eased ever so slightly. Sherry was like that, and despite her decided lack of enthusiasm, it *was* good to see her. To Sherry, life was one nonstop adventure and whenever you spent longer than a minute in her presence, you found yourself wanting in on it. Jason couldn't help but smile, remembering a few of her former antics. His visit may've been libido-prompted by a certain prodigal sister's return, but he was glad he came.

"You know what I mean," Sherry said, tossing him a wink. She plopped down at a table near the bar and pushed out a chair for him to join her. "You're on the friends and family plan, so you don't count as, like, a *real* customer."

"Awesome." Jason smirked as he took the offered seat. "'Cause real customers have to pay."

Sherry slapped her hand over his with a good-hearted grin. "You're not *that* close." She paused a beat and then said, "I kid, I kid. You know your money's no good here, Landry." She shoved his hand away and laughed. "Actually, it's been too long since I've seen your ugly mug around these parts. What brings you to our humble establishment? We're not in violation of any fire codes, are we?"

They both glanced around the empty restaurant and Jason shook his head. "Not that I'm aware of."

"Then are you hungry?"

He shrugged. "I can always eat," he told her truthfully. And if Colby was cooking, he was definitely curious. "But can't a guy just drop by to say hello to his friends?"

Sherry propped her chin in her hand. "He can," she said, her voice taking on her Nancy Drew tone. That had been her favorite series as a kid, and he used to tease that she was a junior detective. Present day Sherry narrowed her eyes. "But you haven't 'just dropped by' in a long time."

"I know." He kicked back in his chair and casually glanced around the room. "That's why I'm here. Where is everyone?"

It took him a few moments to realize Sherry hadn't answered—and silence from Sherry was never a good sign. Jason quickly shifted his attention away from the closed kitchen door to find her watching him, mouth scrunched, eyes clear and intent.

"Cane doesn't come in for another half hour," she said, tapping a painted black nail against the scarred wooden tabletop. *Click, click, click.* "But then, you would've seen his motorcycle wasn't here." *Click.* She switched hands, placing her chin in the opposite hand, and tapped the nails of her free hand in quick succession. *Click, click, click, click.* "Something's definitely up with you," she finally decided, falling back into eerie silence.

Coming there had been a mistake. He should've just gone to the gym like he'd planned, gotten some of his aggression out on the heavy bag before his class started for the night. Instead, he'd chosen to ignore all semblance of logic, and now he'd awoken the sleeping matchmaker.

A *bang* and muffled curse erupted from the kitchen. About ten seconds later, Colby stormed through the pocket door. The dignified linen suit she'd worn at the competition was gone, replaced by a distressed pair of hip-hugging jeans that showed off her impossibly long legs. A soft gray T-shirt clung to the curves of her breasts. As she moved, the generous mounds bounced in rhythm. Her dark hair was piled high on her head, exposing the ivory slope of her neck. Jason swallowed. Any hope he'd held that yesterday's attraction had simply been a symptom of the Louisiana heat was completely decimated.

"Sherry, I swear to God, those take-out containers are going to be the death of me." Colby plowed through the room cradling her left hand to her chest, her face a mask of frustration and pain that disappeared the moment she saw him sitting there. She glanced at her sister across from him and back again. Her mouth tumbled open. "Oh. It's you."

* * *

Colby cringed, lowering her hand to her waist. *Way to go, Captain Obvious.* But seriously, what was Jason doing there? She'd literally just been thinking about him, although that was nothing different from what she'd done ever since yesterday's competition. After a sleepless night and an even more distracted morning, she had hoped the familiarity and busyness of the kitchen would get her mind off the hunky fireman. But while ladling a bowl of to-go gumbo, Colby's mind had wandered to the étouffée she'd sampled the day before. And all the ways she would've preferred awarding Jason for his Best Bite.

Which, when you're dealing with steaming Creole stew, flimsy foam containers, and a chef with a reputation in her family for being less than graceful, wasn't exactly the smartest move. So when her visions had morphed into steamy, NC-17 material, and her thumb jutted through the fragile container, spilling hot gumbo all over her hand, she really had no one but herself to blame.

Awesome.

Then to take it up another notch, she'd stormed out like a whiny child only to find the star of her yummy fantasy sitting in her dining room, dressed in all his civilian glory. Colby, not unlike every other woman on the planet, was a sucker for a man in uniform...but Jason wasn't just any man. The way he filled out a threadbare T-shirt and wind pants was pretty darn amazing, too.

A grin spread across his tan face as he tipped his chair forward. "You know, you're the second woman today to give me that enthusiastic welcome." He sent Sherry a look and then gave Colby a wink. "I must be losing my touch."

Well, hot damn. If this was Jason losing his touch, she didn't think she could handle the man fully on his game.

Colby cleared her throat. "I just wasn't expecting to see you," she explained. "Of course I'm glad you're here." Suddenly feeling edgy and not knowing why, she smoothed back the escaped strands of hair that had fallen from her clip—completely forgetting about the burn she'd inflicted on her hand. When raw skin brushed against the shell of her ear, she flinched and bit off another curse.

"Hey, are you all right?"

Before she could respond or attempt to play it off, Jason covered the distance between them. He gently took her hand in his and frowned at the angry red welt.

"I'm fine," she told him, hating the breathlessness of her voice and hoping he didn't notice. With him standing this close, she could smell the woodsy scent of his cologne. She could feel the warmth coming off his body. It made her head feel fuzzy. Not helping her equilibrium at all was the sight of his strong hands cradling hers. Colby drew a breath, and when the scent of pine hit her, her knees wobbled.

"Really," she tried again, embarrassed over the attention. "It's no big deal. I should've been wearing my chef's jacket." Her cheeks flushed. "It's hanging on a hook on the back of the door. I know better than that. Kitchen burns happen all the time."

But the kitchen had been so dang hot. As hot as it could get in the desert, the dry heat had nothing on New Orleans humidity.

Jason pursed his firm lips together. "Even still, we should get this taken care of." He led her back behind the bar and put the stopper down in the sink, keeping her hand gently clasped in his own. As the basin filled with cool water, he sent her a sympathetic smile. "Where do you keep your first-aid kit?"

At that moment, Colby didn't think she could form a coherent thought, much less answer his question. Could the man be any cuter? Thankfully Sherry, who'd up to this point been content watching their interaction, shot to her feet. "On it." She jogged back behind the bar, pulled out a tackle box filled with supplies, and slid it across the mahogany top. "Here you go, Captain. Stocked to your every detailed specification."

Jason grinned as he gradually immersed Colby's hand in the water. Not letting go of her wrist, he kicked out a waist-high step stool for her to sit on and leaned his hip against the counter. "Let's just hold this in here for a few minutes. I know you probably think it isn't necessary, but it definitely can't hurt."

Colby nodded, still at a loss for words. It had been a long time since she'd let someone take care of her. She had to admit, it felt good.

The cool water did, too.

Her sister walked back around the bar and resumed her position at the table in front of them, not even trying to give them any privacy. Not that she should, since for all Sherry knew, there was no need for them to be alone. Colby met her sister's amused gaze. Her purple-stained lips lifted into a mischievous grin.

Crap, am I that obvious?

Colby rolled her eyes and gave a subtle shake of her head. The last thing she needed was for her baby sister to go all matchmaker on her. Just because Sherry was addicted to love, she thought everyone else should be, too. Sherry hadn't become jaded yet; she had no real reason to be. And Colby sincerely hoped it stayed that way.

She turned her focus back to Jason. "We didn't really get much of a chance to talk yesterday," she said. "*Un*officially, that is."

"No, we didn't," Jason agreed. "You disappeared as soon as the competition was over."

It hadn't been as dramatic as that, but close. First, she'd gone off with Cane and performed the obligatory round of chatting with local officials and potential customers. Then she'd made her swift escape to her recently purchased, very pretty, but highly unpredictable used car.

During the actual competition, Colby had been able to ignore the sad memories whispering in her ear and focus on the task at hand, a feat she largely attributed to the man holding her hand in his warm grasp now. But once the event was over and the crowd had engulfed her with questions of where she'd been and how long she was staying, she'd bolted as soon as humanly possible.

"I had a bit of a headache," she admitted.

Compassion flooded his eyes, softening the color to melted caramel. "I'm sorry to hear that." He turned off the tap and flicked his hand in the water, testing the cool temperature. "But, since I didn't get the chance before, let me now *officially* say on behalf of the fire department and all those privileged to have witnessed your gruesome flannel stage in the nineties, welcome back to Magnolia Springs." He bowed his head in mock reverence. When he lifted it again, he looked directly into her eyes. "We've missed you."

Warmth from the sincere sentiment and playful reminder of her unfortunate former fashion sense flooded her. "I missed you, too."

And she had. Maybe not Jason directly, but what he represented. Whenever Colby came home after a particularly long day to an empty apartment and put her feet up on her Pottery Barn coffee table, she would find herself getting homesick. For her brother, for her sister, and for all the friends she had in Magnolia Springs. Her former unrequited crush included. Just not so much that she wanted to move back permanently.

Jason smiled. The look he gave had her heartbeat thrumming in her throat. Rushing to cover the sentimental moment, she took a step away and said, "Wow, an award-winning chef, a fire captain, and now a member of the Magnolia Springs welcome committee? Why, Mister Landry, you've grown up to be quite multi-talented."

He laughed under his breath. "That I am," he confirmed, his eyes lowering to her lips. "And that's only scratching the surface."

The interior of the room instantly shot up at least ten degrees, despite the limb immersed in cool water. Colby hadn't intended the double meaning to her words—but the added information was good to know.

Very good to know.

Since she'd left the park, Colby had wondered if she had imagined his interest. Made up a mutual flirtation where there had only been adolescent-like gawking on her part. The young guy she'd known would've never looked twice at her. He'd been too focused on his high school girlfriend Ashleigh to notice any other girl within a five-mile radius—especially one with the last name of Robicheaux. But the way Jason was looking at her now erased all of yesterday's concerns.

Not that they're true concerns anyway, she reminded herself, since nothing could ever happen between them. Her heart was officially and forever off the market. Still, it was nice to know that he found her attractive.

"Is that right?" she asked, fighting a smile.

A snort erupted from across the bar. Colby's eyes widened. She'd completely forgotten about their audience.

Sherry paused in her task of wiping down the few tables around them and captured her top lip between her teeth in a silent laugh. Her eyes shined, clearly saying that she knew she'd been forgotten—and that she'd loved every minute of it. She flicked the cloth onto the bar top. "Please," she said, circling her right hand in the air, "do tell us, Jason. What other areas are you talented in?"

The tips of his ears burned red, but that was the only indication he was embarrassed. Colby, on the other hand, wanted to crawl under the cash register. Jason reached out to yank one of her sister's dyed-purple strands. "All I meant was that I also own a gym," he clarified with a good-humored grin before glancing back at Colby. "Northshore Combatives, down at the corner of Main and Wisteria."

"Wait, the old bridal shop?" she asked, surprised when he nodded. "Isn't that space large for a gym?"

Colby knew the place well. It was a bridal shop on steroids. The place was freaking huge. When she was seven, her cousin Missy had forced her to try on every single flower girl dress in the store, and when she was twelve, her second cousin Brooke had decided the Pepto-Bismol taffeta number in the window was divine. In high school, she and her friends had scoured the racks for the perfect homecoming and prom dresses to no avail. It had really come as no shock when she'd learned of the store's demise.

"Not at all." Jason lifted her hand from the water and gently placed a clean towel from the basket onto her arm, blotting at the excess moisture. "Combatives isn't just a gym. You know the big space downstairs, where Dorothy had kept all the wedding stuff?" Colby nodded. "I converted that into three sections, a separate weight room for men and women, and a large studio with the cardio equipment and a rock-climbing wall." He removed the towel and grabbed a roll of sterile gauze from the tackle box. Wrapping the bandage loosely around her hand he said, "And then upstairs, I teach tactical ninjitsu twice a week, but there's a variety of martial arts, aerobics, kids' fitness—we even have groups that train for MMA and Ninja Warrior." He paused to take a breath and grinned. "You should come check it out sometime."

Colby couldn't help but smile at his enthusiasm. "I will," she said automatically, although she doubted she ever would. She had nothing against his gym. It sounded impressive, especially for their small town. But Colby had never been very coordinated. She was the type of girl who was always picked last in P.E. And she looked like a convulsive kangaroo whenever she attempted anything athletic.

But Jason's warm, genuine smile almost had her rethinking her position. What harm could come from giving it a whirl? She could figure out how to walk on a motorized treadmill without falling on her ample backside, couldn't she? Then she remembered the damage she'd done just a few minutes ago in the kitchen, alone, sans exercise balls or any other hazardous sports equipment. Yeah, it was probably safer to stay at home.

"Good," he said, obviously pleased. He secured the end of the gauze and then tapped two aspirin into his open palm. "After this, you should be good to go."

She accepted the pain relievers and downed them with a swig of Coke. "Thank you," she said as she wiped her mouth, genuinely touched at his concern. Over the years, she'd gotten more burns in the kitchen than she could count and normally just put pickle juice on them and kept on trucking. But this was sweet. She had a silly impulse to swipe the bandage and put it in her memory box. Being around this man was obviously harmful to her health. Sure, there was nothing wrong with a little harmless flirtation, but she couldn't let her inner-teen start spinning idealistic dreams for the future.

"I never did ask what brought you in here today. Do you want something from the kitchen?" She waved her freshly bandaged hand in the air and for some reason, he took it again, holding it gently between both of his. Her voice got breathless again as she said, "Thanks to you, I'm as good as new. I'm still in the middle of prepping for the dinner service, but I can whip you up anything you want."

He grinned. "Anything, huh?"

Colby laughed. Apparently, adult Jason was incorrigible. Choosing to sidestep the little landmine he'd presented, she inclined her head and confided, "I happen to be known for my grilled cheese." She lifted her shoulder in a shrug. "Just saying, word on the street is it's the bomb."

Jason chuckled, low and deep. If a sexier sound existed, she was sure she hadn't heard it. "Thanks for the top-secret intel." His eyes moved back to her lips, and the muscles in his neck worked as he swallowed. "But I should probably get going."

Until that moment, Colby hadn't realized how much they had moved during their conversation. Her butt was perched on the very edge of her stool. His body was angled toward her, his muscular leg wedged between hers. Their heads— their *mouths*—were mere inches apart. It wouldn't take much to close the remaining distance between them and steal the kiss she'd thought about since the one they shared during that game of Kiss and Catch—her *first* kiss.

But in all those childhood daydreams, her annoying sister had never been right there, giddily watching from a few feet away.

And her overbearing, protective brother hadn't just walked through the door, hard eyes focused on their little tête-à-tête. Jason relinquished her hand as if it held the Ebola virus.

"Hey man," Jason said, shoving his hand through his dark hair and then into the pocket of his pants as if he no longer knew what to do with it. "It's been a while. Thought I'd come by and see what's going on."

Cane didn't react. He didn't flinch or say a word. He just fixed his stare between the two of them, and Jason glanced at the door beyond. "But you know, Mom mentioned their new AC unit is being delivered today. I should probably run over and make sure the old man doesn't hurt himself installing it." Jason pulled his keys out of the pocket of his wind pants, the metal whispering against the fabric. "We'll have to grab a beer and catch up later in the week, okay?"

Colby had to scoot back on the stool for him to maneuver out from behind the bar; that's how close she had come to straddling the man's thigh. Good gracious, no wonder Sherry had been practically beaming. What it didn't explain was her brother's reaction. Why was he glaring like they'd just had sex on his beloved, gleaming bar top?

Jason edged around Cane, making sure to give her big brother a wide berth. "I'll call you about that beer." At the door, he placed his hand against the glass inset and turned to nod. "Good seeing you, ladies. Try not to break too many hearts until I see you two again."

He gave Colby a soft parting smile and then walked out.

The second the door closed behind Jason's perfect backside, Cane shook his head. "Don't even think about it, Colby."

Chapter Four

When did her love life, or lack thereof, become her brother's concern? Colby watched Cane march to the back office after eliciting his tidbit of unsolicited advice — or had that been an order? — and shook her head, her mind a jumbled mess.

Had all of that really just happened?

She looked to her sister for confirmation. Sherry grinned as if reading her thoughts, then asked in a voice dripping with sweetness, "Tell me, *Coley*, did the desert heat completely fry your brain?"

Colby blinked rapidly, not sure where *that* came from, only knowing that whenever Sherry evoked her nickname, she was up to something. "Excuse me?"

"Oh, don't give me that," Sherry said, giving her a pointed look. "Correct me if I'm wrong, but wasn't that the guy who had a starring role in your childhood diary?" When Colby's mouth fell open at the admission, Sherry shrugged. "Yep, I read every word, thank you very much, and I'm not afraid to admit it. Nancy Drew had nothing on your teenage drama."

She didn't know why she bothered to be surprised. Sure, she'd hidden the blasted thing and practically had to leave herself a map to find it, but Sherry had always been a determined sleuth. Colby shook her head. Besides making it that much harder to squelch the lovey-dovey ideas floating in her baby sister's head, it wasn't that big a deal that Sherry had read her private thoughts. Just embarrassing. But as for terminating those ideas… "I don't know what you're talking about."

"Please," Sherry said. "That man was flirting his ass off, and you didn't jump on that! Are you crazy?" She resumed wiping down the four-top table. "Personally, I think of Jason as nothing more than an honorary annoying brother. But if that man ever looked at *me* with that level of intensity, I would take him in the back and invent a new use for the spatula."

Colby wrinkled her nose. "What in the heck can you do with a spatula?"

Her sister slid her a cheeky grin. "I don't know. But it would be fun to find out." She looked over the polished tables, nodded, and then slid her bottom onto a barstool with a sigh. "Seriously, Colby, the heat coming from the pair of you could've set off the fire detectors. I kinda felt like a Peeping Tom, to be honest, but there was no way on earth I was missing *that* show." She poked Colby in the arm. "And you, dear sister, are avoiding the question."

Colby shook her head. She grabbed the roll of gauze and bottle of aspirin and returned them to the first-aid kit. "That was just harmless fun." Sherry snorted.

Sliding the tackle box back under the bar, she grabbed her sister's discarded dusting cloth and began rubbing the already gleaming surface. Sherry's distorted reflection appeared beside her on the reddish-brown wood.

"It seems to me like the real fun is still to come," she said in a sort of sing-song voice. Grabbing the clipboard holding the inventory checklist, she skimmed her hand over the bottles of Jim, Jack, and Old Granddad, a playful smile twitching her lips. "You've been given a gift here, Colby. A chance to have a fling with a hot firefighter—what woman wouldn't want that? It's your duty, on behalf of single women everywhere, to pursue this opportunity."

"On behalf of women everywhere?" Colby asked sardonically. "Laying it on kinda thick there, don't you think?"

Sherry huffed and slid her a look of exasperation. "Okay then, do it for me. Your poor sister who hasn't gone out with a halfway decent guy in months, and who hasn't gotten any *good* late-night action since Simon was still judging *American Idol.*" At Colby's pursed lips of skepticism, she clarified. "Don't get me wrong, I've gotten some. Just nothing that great. Listen, Colby, I know you've sworn off men and everything"—Sherry rolled her eyes at the crazy notion—"but you didn't swear off *fun*, did you?"

No, Colby thought, her resolve crumpling. She hadn't. And the last time *she'd* gotten any good late night loving, the country had had a different president.

Life in the restaurant business, especially in Las Vegas, was hectic. Colby was single-handedly responsible for the management of the kitchen, keeping track of inventory, creating dishes, and being the overall creative force behind the entire establishment. Most days kept her so busy that when she did finally slip between the sheets, she was too exhausted to complain that she was doing it alone. But then there were other nights. Nights spent with a glass of red wine in hand and way too much unoccupied space left in her king-sized bed. Nights when she got lonely.

Vowing off relationships didn't mean Colby had taken a vow of chastity, after all. Her sister was right; she was still a woman with needs. A woman who needed a little no-strings-attached fun now and then.

And there was no doubt that a fling with Jason would be *fun*.

Colby bit her lip, but her smile sprung free anyway. Beside her, Sherry began a happy shimmy, already sensing victory. Colby laughed and gave her sister a one-armed hug. "You know, sis, out of all your hare-brained, free-love notions, I have to say this one is my favorite."

Northshore Combatives was loud, hot, and full of sweaty men. The sight fanned the flame of Colby's already fiery libido, but there was only one sweaty man she hoped to see tonight. The man she'd fantasized about all day. Fantasies she planned to make a reality that night. Ever since Sherry put the crazy idea in her head, she couldn't stop imagining Jason in her bed. Between the sheets. Doing the horizontal tango.

It had really been a while.

The one dark cloud in her plan was Cane. He'd put his metaphorical motorcycle boot down, and though she was a grown woman, she wasn't looking to start a sibling feud this summer. She was home for three short months. After being gone for twelve years, she wanted to keep it light and drama free, which meant Cane could never know about her fling with the fireman. But with little sister on big brother watch, keeping him busy at the restaurant so her plan went without interruption, Colby was eager to get a jump on it—excusing the suggestive pun—before she lost her nerve.

That night's dinner service had to have been the longest ever recorded in history. Colby had expected there to be a transition period when she'd taken over the kitchen at Robicheaux's—any change, much less one in a high-stress job, required a little grace. And after a couple weeks of stumbles, she and her staff were finally starting to find their rhythm. Colby had trained up the existing staff and hired Rhonda, who was proving to be a more than competent sous-chef.

But after Jason's visit earlier that day, Colby's mind had been consumed with thoughts of her childhood crush—and wondering how he'd react to her planned activities for the night. Throughout the first dinner service, she had been twitchy, careless, and snippy. And by seven o'clock, Rhonda had given her a good-natured shove out the door. A half hour later, after a quick detour for a shower, Colby had been back on the road headed to Jason's gym. So she could proposition the owner.

What did one say when propositioning a man for a fling, anyway?

Hey hot stuff, wanna knock some boots?

Yeah, she didn't think so, either.

As she looked around the semi-crowded building, Colby fiddled with the strap on her top. She'd come dressed to impress, to seduce. But standing in the middle of a gym filled with half-naked people, wearing her sexiest jeans and a new silk camisole, made her feel like some sort of beacon, signaling she was there to get laid. She checked her watch. Maybe she should just wait in the car.

She turned back in the direction she'd come, promising herself that this was not her chickening out, and a flash of blond caught her eye. A young preteen with a high ponytail and a mouthful of shiny braces was manning the front desk, winding the cord of an ancient-style phone around her finger. Colby realized it was the girl from the park—the one playing Kiss and Catch. The young girl slung her head back in a bark of laughter, and the sound was so natural and spontaneous that Colby found herself hesitating by the door, smiling.

"She did *not* say that!" The young girl pounded her fist

against the textbook lying open on the desktop. "Really? Omigod, that is hi*lar*ious. And then what did Brad say when—" The animated dialogue broke off as the girl spotted Colby lingering, and her smile widened. "Omigod, I gotta go!" Slamming the phone down in its cradle, she targeted her immense energy in Colby's direction. "You're Colby Robicheaux."

It was a statement, not a question. And taken aback, Colby nodded slowly. "I am."

Since working her way up in her career, she had become accustomed to foodies in culinary circles recognizing her. And since returning home, she'd gotten used to the older locals stopping her on the road, remembering her from when she was a kid. But this girl was just a kid herself.

"Wow. It is *such* an honor to meet you." The girl scooted the rolling chair forward and leaned across the desktop. "I Googled you yesterday, after the competition? Your restaurant in Vegas looks amazing, with all those lights and windows— I'm kinda obsessed with restaurants. And the Food Network. Pretty much anything that has to do with cooking. I wanna be a chef, too, one day."

Two red splotches appeared high on the girl's cheeks as she paused to take a breath. That endearing blush, combined with the look in her eyes, full of life and hope, totally stole Colby's heart. It reminded her of how she used to be at that age. But surprisingly, the similarity wasn't painful.

"Oh, I'm Emma, by the way."

Colby smiled. "It's a pleasure to meet you, Emma. And I have to tell you, I'm also addicted to the Food Network." She leaned in as if to impart a secret and the girl put her elbows onto the counter and bent closer, too. "In fact, I have a total food crush on Bobby Flay," she shared with a grin. "And I actually met Giada a few times."

"Shut up!" Emma threw back in the chair and Colby laughed, feeling lighter than she had in a long time. Hanging around with kids tended to do that. "Gosh, that's so awesome," Emma continued. "I can't believe Uncle Cane never mentioned that to me before."

And just like that, Colby's laughter died in her throat.

Sure that she must have heard wrong, she asked, "I'm sorry, did you say *Uncle* Cane?"

Emma's ponytail bounced as she nodded enthusiastically.

Knowing it was highly unlikely another man named after sugarcane had moved to their small town in her absence, but needing to be sure, she added, "Cane Robicheaux? As in my brother?"

"Yep! Well, he's not my *real* uncle, as you'd know. But he's my godfather. He and my dad have been friends for, like, ever."

A sinking sense of horror settled in Colby's gut.

It couldn't be possible…

"Your dad, huh?" she asked, hoping—*praying*—that she was wrong. Fate wouldn't be so cruel. "Does he, ah, happen to own this gym?"

This elicited a beaming smile of pride from the preteen bag of bombshells—and confirmed Colby's worse nightmare. "Yep, that's him. Jason Landry. He's also the fire captain." Emma tilted her head to the side. "I guess if Uncle Cane's your brother, then you must've known my dad when you were younger, too, huh?"

"Oh, I knew him all right," Colby agreed, her head spinning with confusion. *Just not nearly as well as I had thought.*

Jason was married. It was as if her past was coming back to haunt her with a vengeance. The man she thought she knew had flirted with her, had come to her place of work and taken care of her injury with that damn sexy smile on his face, and then gone home to his *family*.

What kind of man did that?

Actually, Colby knew exactly what kind of man—her father. And to a lesser extent, her college ex-boyfriend. *Faithfulness* was a pretty word, but one that she'd learned at a young age wasn't real. Not in her experience. It was after discovering their infidelities back-to-back that Colby had sworn off relationships. And now, twelve years later, it was coming around full-circle. Never would she have thought Jason would be like either of those men...or that one day, she would come this close to becoming the other woman.

Colby rubbed her forehead, feeling a migraine coming on. She was going to kill her baby sister.

"Miss Robicheaux, are you okay?"

How could Sherry have let her walk into this situation? The whole stupid fling idea had been hers in the first place. Did she honestly not know Jason was married? And how could Colby not notice a ring on his finger? After all the time she'd spent staring at the man's hands, you'd think she would've spotted a significant detail like that. She mindlessly grabbed for her phone in her purse.

"Miss Robicheaux?" Emma asked again, concern creeping into her voice.

Colby took a breath and slowly let it out. She held a finger up as she autodialed her sister's number, sending Emma a thin-lipped smile. This wasn't the girl's fault; if anything, she was the victim...or the almost victim.

On the other end, Sherry's phone rang and rang before her perky voice picked up. "Hey, it's me, you know the drill." *Beep.*

"We have to talk," Colby said through gritted teeth. She ended the call and put her phone back in her purse, turning to give Emma a forced smile.

"I'm fine, sweetie," she lied, taking in the young girl's look of concern. "Just seem to be getting a lot of headaches lately."

"Ouch, those suck," Emma said sympathetically. Then her tiny face lit up. "Hey, since you grew up with Dad, does that mean you knew my mom, too?"

A vein throbbed behind Colby's eye. This wasn't just a migraine. Her head was literally going to explode.

Turning to cast a longing glance at her awaiting, temperamental Altima, wanting desperately to be anywhere but here, she kept her tight-lipped smile in place and nodded. Now that she knew what she was looking for, the girl's resemblance to Ashleigh was uncanny. And with Jason, there really was only one person it could be. "Yes I knew her, but not well," she admitted. "I didn't even know your parents got married. It must have happened after I moved away."

Like, right after, now that she thought about it. Colby tilted her head, quickly doing the math. Emma appeared to be about eleven, maybe twelve years old. That meant she'd been born around the same time Colby had moved to New York for culinary school. She didn't think Jason was married to Ashleigh when she left, but by then, he and Cane had been at Louisiana Tech in Ruston.

Emma's incandescent glow dimmed slightly. Shrugging her thin shoulders she said, "That's all right. I just love talking to people who knew her, you know? I don't remember much. I was only seven when she died."

It took a moment for the words and their meaning to sink in. Colby was too busy trying to fill in the back-story and plan her current escape route. But when they did, her stomach bottomed out. And she felt about *this* big.

Of course Jason wasn't married. He was a widower. It hadn't even occurred to her that could be an option. Or even, now that her head was a little clearer, that he could've been divorced. She had been so quick to assume the worst about him. To only see the situation through the lens of her past.

Guilt and compassion washed over her. And even a shade of sorrow for Ashleigh. She hadn't been close to Jason's girlfriend; Ashleigh had been older, and she'd been the recipient of the one thing a young Colby wanted more than anything—Jason's affections. But she never wished harm on the beautiful woman.

"I'm so sorry," she told Emma, knowing from experience what little comfort words can really be. Swallowing past the ache in her throat, Colby leaned against the desk and touched Emma's hand. "It's never easy when you lose a parent. I lost my mom in a car accident a few years ago."

The girl squeezed Colby's hand and her big brown eyes— eyes that Colby now realized resembled her father's—filled with sympathy. "And then your dad just a few months ago. Wow, I can't imagine losing Dad, too. That must be so sad." Her gentle squeeze became a compassionate pat. "It's good that you're around family now," she said sagely, sounding at least thirty years old. Maybe even older.

Despite the emotions roiling in her stomach, Colby had to fight back a smile. "Yes, it is," she agreed with a nod. Then she looked around the gym again. Now that her night's agenda was out the window—there was no way she was propositioning a man for sex when he was on homework duty—she didn't really know what to do with herself.

While she supposed there were some widowers with children who had wild and crazy flings, he didn't seem like the type. He'd want more, a commitment. And that was simply off the table for her. Plus, she'd been the confused girl in the middle before. While two single people having a casual fling was not the same as an extra-marital affair, Colby knew

Emma could get hurt. And she'd been through way too much in her young life for that.

With a sigh she said, "You know, Emma, I just remembered I forgot something at the restaurant." She grabbed her keys from her purse and lifted her hand in a wave. "It was nice meeting you."

"You, too, Miss Robicheaux," Emma said, smiling wide. "And I'll be sure to tell Dad you stopped by!"

Colby's face twisted in a grimace. She'd honestly rather the young girl didn't, but what possible reason could she give to refuse? "Thanks, Emma. That would be great."

. . .

"She stopped by to say hello?" Jason asked, flipping on the light as he walked through the door of his Acadian-style home. He was exhausted, in bad need of a shower, and a peanut butter protein shake was calling his name. But it figured his daughter would wait until right after he'd put the key in the door to mention Colby's visit. "Just hello? That was all she said?"

Emma shrugged. "Pretty much. We talked about the restaurant and cooking— Hey, did you know she's actually met Giada? Like, more than once. Isn't that awesome?"

Jason loved his daughter. He did. She was smart and funny. She could kick a boy's ass climbing a tree and then come home and bake a killer lasagna. But sometimes, following her train of thought was kind of like trying to navigate through a spider web. "That *is* awesome, Em. But did Colby say anything about why she came by? Ask about the gym, or a trial membership?"

She shook her head. "No. But you know, now that you mention it, she wasn't really dressed to work out. She had on a cool pair of jeans and a fancy shirt. And lots of makeup." She smiled. "She looked pretty."

Jason figured that was a given. But he'd seen Colby earlier that day, and knew she had worked that night. He doubted she'd bother changing into a fancy shirt only to hide it under a chef's jacket. And none of it explained why she would drive blocks out of her way just to turn around before seeing him. Especially after that look Cane had nailed them both with that afternoon. "Did she at least take a class schedule?"

"Nope. She came in, we chatted, she left." Emma shrugged. "Actually, she looked kinda surprised to meet me. I guess she didn't expect me to be there."

Or knew that you existed, Jason thought with a wince.

He didn't know why he hadn't mentioned Emma before. It wasn't as if she were a secret. She just hadn't come up as a topic in their brief bits of conversation. He guessed it was possible Cane had told her about his spunky godchild, but he doubted it. His friend wasn't exactly known for his verboseness.

Emma dropped her school bag onto the dining room table and headed for the pantry. After setting the ingredients for his post-workout shake on the counter, she grabbed a box of raisins for herself. Jason smiled, switching back into full-on parent mode.

"Homework?" he asked, beginning the nightly inquisition.

"Done. Even diagramming." She made a face.

"Very good. Dirty clothes?"

"Already waiting in the laundry room," she said with a nod. "Leftovers put away. Sink empty. Snackage in hand."

"That's my girl." He walked up to give her a hug, but she wrinkled her nose at his sweaty shirt. Instead, he put out his palm for a high-five. "All right, go take your shower and lights out in an hour. Deal?"

She slapped his hand and took off in a flash of bouncing

blond hair. Jason laughed as he grabbed the carton of milk from the fridge. There were definitely things that Emma needed, questions she had that required a woman's touch, but he also knew that so far he'd done a damn good job on his own. Emma was a smart kid with great grades. She had friends and fun, but still helped around the house. She even pitched in a couple hours a week at the gym. If he didn't marry again, she would turn out just fine—but Jason wanted *more* than fine for his daughter. He wanted her secure and confident. He wanted her well-rounded. He wanted to give her everything she deserved. And right now, he believed that was a mother.

The problem was, of course, finding one. One that wouldn't split the moment she found out he was a single father—as Colby had apparently done earlier—or want more than he was willing to give. He'd already suffered one major heartbreak in his life; he had no interest in signing on for another.

After finishing his shake and rinsing out the blender, Jason stopped in the laundry room to start another load. Emma exited the bathroom as he passed, pink-cheeked and dressed in ice cream pajamas.

"Hey Dad," she said, leaning against the doorjamb. "I was thinking."

Jason froze in his tracks. In his experience, when a woman uttered those words, it was rarely a good sign. "Oh yeah?" he asked. "What about?"

"Miss Robicheaux. I think you should ask her out."

He blinked. He flicked his gaze toward the wedding photo hanging near the doorway, then raised an eyebrow. "You do, huh?"

"Yeah," she said, gathering her damp hair for her ever-present ponytail. "You're cute—or at least my friends say you are." She curled her lip and made a gagging noise. "And you're still young. For the most part, anyway. Miss Robicheaux seemed nice, and she's pretty. I think you should ask her out." Hair in place, Emma yanked an elastic hair tie off her wrist and wrapped it around twice. "Think about it."

She stood on tiptoe and kissed his cheek. Then she scooted into her bedroom and closed the door, leaving Jason gobsmacked in the hall.

Chapter Five

Who needed men or a steamy fling when you could eat your weight in chocolate? That's what Colby wanted to know as she walked down the aisle of sugary goodness at Trosclair's Convenience Store. Chocolate had never steered her wrong in the past. It added some extra padding to her backside, yes. But when your life plan was to end up an old maid who apparently couldn't *find* her boots, much less knock any, then a detail like that shouldn't matter.

"Bitterness doesn't become you, Colby," she muttered as she grabbed a king-sized Hershey's with almonds. Not propositioning Jason had been *her* decision. But even though it had been the right one, it didn't make the past two nights any less lonely. Or less filled with erotic dreams of what could've been. Thinking better of it, Colby turned back to the shelf and grabbed a Kit-Kat, too. Glancing at the items in her hands, she mentally counted backward approximately twenty-eight days.

Hmm. Apparently being denied a sweaty session between the sheets with Jason wasn't the only thing making her moody. It was entirely possible she was also suffering from PMS.

"Oh joy," she muttered again, waving as she passed old

Mrs. Thibodeaux on her way toward the feminine hygiene section. The kind, gray-haired woman lifted a weathered hand in return.

In Vegas, Colby could've gone an entire month, maybe longer, without recognizing anyone during her errands. It made shopping on bad hair days easy. But in Magnolia Springs, she was lucky to grab the mail without someone stopping her on the street for a chat. Not in the mood to reminisce while contemplating periods and chocolate, Colby picked up her pace.

As she neared the row in question, she heard a familiar, spunky voice.

"Dad, this is *epically* embarrassing. Can't we just pick something—anything—and go?"

Colby cringed. In those few words, she was able to get the entire picture in her mind. The anguished tone of Emma's voice only heightened the image. And judging by the girl's age, Colby would bet even money they were dealing with a monumental first. One that a guy, no matter how hard he tried, would never understand.

She rounded the corner and sure enough, there stood a distraught-looking Jason, ankle deep in boxes of tampons and pads. He held a box of each at eye level. "They make different products for a reason, Bug," he said, reading the back of one intently. "I only wish I knew when you needed what. Ultra-Thin, Super Long, Regular, Heavy." He glanced at his daughter. "Do you know how heavy your flow is?"

Colby slapped a hand over her mouth. Oh, the poor man did not just ask her that.

Emma's eyes widened, and Colby could see the words *Oh, make this stop* floating in her mind. Colby was far from motherly, but she certainly couldn't do worse than Jason at the moment, bless his good-intentioned heart. Deciding it was best for everyone involved if she stepped in as soon as possible, Colby strode toward them. "Hey guys, what's up?"

Two pairs of matching brown eyes turned to her in relief. Jason mouthed the words, "Help me," and Colby sent him a subtle nod. Turning to the distressed adolescent, she said, "It's nice to see you again, Emma."

"Miss Robicheaux, you have *no idea* how good it is to see you." The girl lifted her eyebrows and gave the box of maxi pads at her feet a pointed look.

Knowing how touchy this subject could be, but not wanting to overstep any boundaries either, Colby turned to the row of options and selected her go-to brand of tampons. Normally, hygiene products were a taboo subject that she went out of her way to avoid around men. Whenever male visitors came over, she hid them deep in the back of her cabinets. But this was not the time to be squeamish. All three of them knew how female plumbing worked. And this situation was bigger than silly awkwardness.

She turned to find both of them studying her selection with fascination.

Maybe it *wasn't* bigger.

Her eyes fell to the box in her hands, her fingers tightening around the cardboard. Making a big deal about this would only embarrass Emma more, but suddenly, Colby was eleven years old again.

She would *never* forget that cold January night. It was the stuff nightmares were made of—or at least, the nightmares of lovesick adolescents. It was the night of Sherry's ballet recital, and they'd all been running around like chickens with their heads cut off. Knowing that Jason was coming with them, Colby had made the last-minute decision to jump in the shower, hoping a fresh shampoo of her hair would be just the thing to get him to notice her.

He'd noticed her all right. In fact, he'd gotten two big eyefuls of her freshly scrubbed, prepubescent naked backside. Fresh from the shower, she'd been ass in the air rummaging through a cabinet for the very items in her hand when Jason opened the door. She'd frozen in place, the box hit the floor with a resounding *smack*, and then…he'd laughed.

It was *awesome*.

"Gentle glide," Emma read from the bright pink box. "That makes sense."

Jason grabbed a box of it too, and added it to the mountain at his feet.

Colby smiled as he scratched his stubbled jawline and surveyed the products, clearly out of his element. "Honestly, this stuff is more about personal preference than anything. Emma, if I were you, I'd start with these Tween pads. They're made for girls your age." She bent to pick up one of Jason's boxes, along with a larger one beside it. "And just in case, I'd get this variety pack, too."

Emma nodded and Jason took the items gratefully. He topped it off by adding a bottle of Midol to the items in his arms. All the man needed was a box of brownies and he'd be a walking advertisement for Kotex.

Watching the two of them together, Colby thought back to the day she'd gotten *her* first period. It had been Mother's Day, oddly enough, and in the middle of church. When her mother discovered what had happened, she canceled her annual brunch, told the boys to go do manly things, and took Colby and Sherry out for a woman's day. She turned a mortifying day into one that remained one of Colby's most treasured memories. And suddenly, that was what she wanted to do for Emma.

"You know," she said carefully, unsure if she should intrude on their moment, "Wednesdays are typically slower at the restaurant. I'm off today and was just on my way home for an afternoon of vegging on the sofa, watching Food Network, and stuffing my face full of chocolate."

She wasn't sure which made Emma's eyes sparkle more—the proposed viewing schedule, or the bars of chocolate in her hand.

Stifling a grin, she turned to address the girl's handsome father. "I take it Emma is out of school now?"

Jason nodded. "She got excused at recess after—" Emma's lips pinched together and he trailed off. "Ah, she's off today for medical reasons."

His daughter groaned and threw her head into her hands. Jason grimaced. It was obvious the man was trying. Anyone could see that. But he was dealing with a hormonal preteen, and he was a man. Pretty much anything he said right now would be considered embarrassing.

"That works, then," Colby said, continuing with her plan. "Sherry has to work tonight, and I hate eating chocolate alone."

Besides, Colby wasn't sure she was ready to forgive her sister yet for leaving out the vital detail that Jason had a child. Sherry swore she hadn't mentioned Emma because she didn't think it would make a difference...but Colby had caught the glint in her eye. Her cupid-sister *knew*—or had a decent-sized hunch—that a kid could've been a deal-breaker, and Sherry was nothing if not determined.

Returning her full attention to the present situation, Colby gave Emma a very serious look. "Don't get me wrong; I don't share my chocolate." She winked and the preteen grinned. "Anyone who hangs with me has to have her own stash. But consuming copious amounts of calories doesn't feel so pathetic when you have company." She glanced at Jason, who gave a subtle nod, and then transferred her gaze back to

Emma. "Any chance you'd like to join me?"

The exhale of relief, from both Landrys, was audible. Emma turned to her father with a pleading look, and Jason bit off a smile. "I think that could be arranged," he said, chuckling as his daughter's shoulders sagged in dramatic relief. "But you still have to finish your math assignment," he added. "And be home by seven."

"Totally," she answered, slinging her arms around his waist in a tight hug. Over his daughter's head, Jason slid Colby the most beautiful smile she'd ever seen.

Her insides turned to molten lava. For the better part of the last thirty years, she had lusted after the man in front of her. She'd seen him at the breakfast table with adorable bedhead. She'd seen him dressed up and smelling good, heading to a party. Colby had seen Jason at all ages and stages of his life—heck, she even saw him in his hero getup a few days ago. But without question, he had never looked more attractive than he did in that moment. Standing in the middle of a drug store aisle, surrounded by tampons, and holding his daughter after trying so hard to help her.

Colby wasn't interested in dating a dad or becoming a surrogate mother; heck, the thought of being responsible for molding a young mind gave her hives. But even *she* could admit that Jason made fatherhood look good.

And that was cosmically unfair.

Seeing Jason again had sparked all her childhood feelings, feelings that her sister had kicked into overdrive with her unhelpful suggestion of a fling. Now Colby was afraid a simple roll in the hay wouldn't be enough. And it would have to be. At the end of the summer, she was moving back to Vegas. But the two of them could be friends. All three of them, actually. And it was even possible that hanging around Jason with his daughter in tow would help the desire to tackle the man and drag him to her bed subside.

It was unlikely, but it was definitely worth a shot.

Later that night, after an afternoon filled with culinary television, the best batch of chocolate chip cookies the world had ever seen, and endless advice on feminine supplies, Colby drove Emma back home. It was storming, and water pounded the windshield as she pulled into their circular driveway. Rivulets of rain cascaded down the gables on the sloped roof and gushed out the downspout of the gutter in front of them. It was so not the right weather for a white shirt.

Grabbing an umbrella, Colby jogged around the front of the car, her feet splashing in the instant puddles. Emma grabbed her enormous backpack and together they sloshed up the paved drive.

Before they'd made it to the red brick steps, Jason threw open the door. "Come in," he said, his voice muffled by the rain beating against the roof. Wrapping a hand around Colby's elbow, he dragged her inside, Emma squeezing in behind her. Jason took the umbrella from her hands and held it outside the open door, shaking off the water. "Stay for a few minutes while it dies down out there."

Cool air-conditioning kissed her wet skin and she shivered. But the response had as much to do with the man standing beside her as it did the temperature. With his feet bare and damp, coal black hair curling around his ears, it was obvious Jason had just stepped out of the shower. The clean scent of soap wafted off his skin. His MSFD T-shirt stretched over his broad shoulders and his jeans hung low on his hips. The desire to lick a trail from the bottom of his feet to the top of his head was so strong, her knees wobbled. She glanced at

Emma, and as hoped, the effect was like an immediate cold shower. *Get your hormones in line, girl.*

Swiping away the moisture on her face, Colby pinched the fabric of her own T-shirt and unstuck it from her body. Even without the aid of a mirror, she was confident she looked like a drowned rat. "Guess umbrellas are pointless when the rain comes down sideways, huh?"

Jason laughed. After setting the umbrella in the holder on the covered porch, he closed the door and said, "The storm should pass over soon. Why don't you stay for dinner? I just finished getting it ready, and while I might not own a big time restaurant or anything, you happen to be looking at an award-winning chef."

"Oh, is that right?" Colby shot Emma a sly grin and said, "You should know, I heard through the grapevine that the judge from the other day has horrible taste. I wouldn't put much stock in her opinion if I were you."

Emma's eyes darted between them, an excited smile on her face. "But you'll stay, though, right?" she asked enthusiastically, the same way she did pretty much everything. "You can tell Dad about all the celebrities who've come into your restaurant!"

Feeling cornered, Colby said, "Well, maybe…" She snuck a quick breath and inhaled the distinct aroma of oregano and basil. *Italian.* She was in luck. With an exaggerated sigh, she relented. "I guess you two wore me down."

Jason held his palm up, and Emma slapped it. "No one can deny a Landry," he told his daughter.

And that's what worries me. Grown-up Jason had a playful side, one that Colby liked a lot. Maybe too much. "Do you two mind if I freshen up first?"

"Not at all," he said, inclining his head for her to follow. She kicked off her shoes and padded across the soft carpet through the open living room. A black leather sectional sofa dominated the space, along with a wall-mounted television and a coffee table littered with what appeared to be a strange mix of various martial art and teen magazines. Frames on the walls displayed the passing years of Emma's life, and in the middle of the focal wall, a family photograph showed a gap-toothed girl surrounded by her adoring parents.

Colby wanted to stop and study the picture, but she kept on moving. She didn't want to upset Emma. And she didn't want to ruin the light-hearted mood that had fallen over the room. Stealing a final glance at the cozy family unit, she followed Jason into his rather large kitchen, outfitted with stainless steel appliances. She could imagine father and daughter working together in the roomy space, laughing, cooking together, creating…much like *she* used to do with her dad.

Nope, not gonna happen. Colby shut down the thought before it could go any further. Thoughts of her past weren't going to ruin the night, either.

Jason stopped in front of the gas stove. "Emma, why don't you show Colby the way to the bathroom? Maybe change out of those wet clothes while you're at it."

"On it." She took Colby's hand and led her through a rounded door into another hallway lined with frames.

"Someone is certainly photogenic," Colby said, smiling at an eight-by-ten school photo of Emma, trademark ponytail in place.

"Yeah, Mom was a photo nut," Emma explained. "I think Dad's afraid to take anything down, like it's going to upset me or something. So he just keeps adding new pictures to the walls. Soon he's gonna have to hang them on the ceiling." She pushed open a door and pointed inside. "This is the bathroom. My dad's room is at the end of the hall, the laundry room is on the other, and here's my room," she said, indicating the closed door across from the bathroom. Turning the knob exposed a sea of blue walls and a matching bedspread. "Just holler if you need anything." Then Emma ducked inside and closed the door.

Colby turned back to the bathroom. She needed to clean herself up, and try to get a handle on the wet mess otherwise known as her hair. But the large wedding photograph she just spied at the end of the hallway was calling her name. If she was quiet, she could slip down the hall now and get a good, unaccompanied stare at Ashleigh on her wedding day, and the look in Jason's eye she already knew she'd find when he gazed at her. With a quick glance in either direction, Colby sprinted across the plush carpet and toward the gilded frame.

Ashleigh had been tall, blond, and gorgeous. Basically everything Colby wasn't. In the picture, she stared up at her new husband, obviously head over heels in love. Like she did back in high school. Colby had only been a freshman when they were seniors, but she used to watch them from across the cafeteria. They were the golden couple, and Jason loved surprising his girl with a single flower or a box of candy. Little things that fueled Colby's fantasies. And every time he brought those gifts, Ashleigh would look up at him with the same expression of love she did in their wedding photo.

As for the groom, the Jason in the photograph was the Jason that Colby remembered from her childhood. Young and handsome, with that mischievous glint in his expressive eyes. His dark hair was longer then. Studying him closer, Colby decided he couldn't be older than early twenties; she'd say twenty-one or twenty-two at the most. A love-struck smile tugged at young Jason's lips, and an irrational sense of jealousy flared in her gut.

Turning back to Ashleigh, Colby glimpsed what Emma

would look like in about ten years. While the girl had Jason's eyes, the rest was clearly all Mama. From her height, to her smile, to the color of her hair, Emma had to be a daily reminder of Jason's deceased wife.

How painful must that be?

Knowing her time was running short, she took another step closer to the picture, soaking up every detail in pathetic curiosity. The way Jason held her hand, the way he looked at his wife, the old-fashioned style of the bride's wedding dress...

Colby narrowed her eyes, zeroing in on how the gown flared at the bride's stomach.

Unless she was mistaken, that was a decided baby bump. Another piece fell into place.

A *thump* sounded from inside Emma's bedroom. Not wanting to be caught snooping, Colby flew down the hall and enclosed herself in the bathroom.

• • •

"I guess that judge knew what she was talking about after all," Colby declared, slapping her hands over her flat stomach. Jason averted his eyes from the sexy flash of skin. *What is wrong with me?* "Because that pasta was positively delicious. Well done, Chef Landry. You'd give me a run for my money any day."

He nodded his thanks, grateful for the compliment, as unlikely as it may be. He'd cooked many meals in his life. Even before Ashleigh died, he'd enjoyed tooling around in the kitchen. Focusing on the tasks of chopping, stirring, and adding the occasional random spice to the recipe he was using quieted his overactive mind. And after becoming a widower and the sole provider for his daughter's daily nutrition, well, that enjoyment turned into more than just a hobby. As Emma grew older, sharing that time with her, watching cooking shows and inventing new recipes, brought them closer. Jason had definitely learned a lot about food in the last few years… but a restaurant quality chef he'd never be.

"Coming from you, that is high praise indeed. But had I remembered your restaurant in Vegas was Italian, I might've been too intimidated to ask you to stay."

Colby laughed, a soft, musical sound that made him smile. And tonight, he'd heard it a lot. Between her jabs at him for his Zack Morris fade haircut, his digs at her about her metal mouth years, and Emma teasing them both for their "weird" taste in music, the night had been comfortable and fun. Dinner had always been a special time for him and Emma, a natural extension of their mutual love of cooking. Whenever he was off-duty, they would eat together at the table, catching up on the highs and lows of each other's days. Truth be told, it was his favorite part of the day. He hadn't thought it could get any better. Tonight, Colby proved him wrong.

In so many ways, she was *exactly* what he was looking for.
 But Colby wasn't for him.

That was what he had to keep reminding himself. If Cane's obvious opposition wasn't enough, during dinner Colby had revealed her plan to leave at the end of the summer. Regardless of how well she seemed to *fit*, pursuing her to become Emma's stepmother was not an option.

"Emma told me earlier that she makes a mean lasagna, too," Colby said, tossing his daughter a smile. "I told her I could use a good set of helping hands in the kitchen. I was thinking she could maybe come by the restaurant after school on Friday and be my junior sous-chef."

Emma squealed, and they both laughed.

"Clearly, she has no interest whatsoever," Jason said, giving her ponytail a playful yank. It was obvious she wanted to spend as much time with Colby as she could. Part of him worried about her getting too attached, knowing Colby would be leaving in three short months. But spending time inside a real restaurant kitchen beside a *real* chef would be an amazing opportunity for his daughter. One that he couldn't keep her from experiencing. "I'm at the station that day," he said, "but I'm sure my mom can drop her by after school."

"Oh, how is your mom?" Colby leaned forward, setting her elbows on the table with genuine interest.

Jason grinned. "Mom's good. She's retired now, her and my dad both. She still helps at the school as a substitute now and then, but mostly she spends her days reading romance novels and helping with Emma when I'm working a shift."

"Emma, your grandmother is the reason I started reading anything other than recipes. She was hands down the best teacher at Magnolia Springs Elementary." Looking back at Jason, she said, "But while I'd love to see your mom again, Emma could always come by on Saturday if it's easier."

"I can't," Emma broke in, setting down her glass of milk. "That's my birthday camping trip. Actually, my birthday isn't until next Thursday, but this year it's a golden one—you know, when your birth date and age match? So Dad said that I could pick *anything* I wanted to do—"

"Anything within reason," Jason amended with a grin.

Emma rolled her eyes, as if she wouldn't have asked for a trip to New York had he not added that stipulation, and continued. "*Anything* I wanted, and I've never been camping before." Then a strange expression crossed over her face and her lips twitched. Colby shot Jason a look.

"You just said *anything* within reason, right, Dad?" Emma asked. Jason slowly nodded, curious as to why she kept emphasizing that word, and Emma slid their dinner guest an innocent, wide-eyed grin. "Then could you join us, Colby?"

Jason hadn't been expecting that. And from the panicked look on Colby's face, neither had she.

"U-Uh," she stammered, taking her napkin off her lap and placing it on the plate in front of her. She licked her lips and sent him an unidentifiable look. "Well, Emma, I'm honored you want me to be a part of your special day," she said carefully. "But wouldn't I be intruding?"

Jason couldn't tell by the look on her face if she wanted an out or not. And he still wasn't sure if he should encourage Emma's hero worship. But the more Jason thought about it, the more he realized that he wanted Colby there. Emma deserved a special birthday. She deserved a dozen of them. And within reason, he wanted to give her everything she asked for. If Colby's presence made her day that much better, that was what he wanted to give her. Plus, he'd be lying if he said he didn't like the idea of spending more time with the enchanting chef himself.

So he answered honestly. "You wouldn't be intruding at all. We're just going down the street to LeBeaux Park for the night. Walk a few trails, roast a few hot dogs, and eat a few dozen s'mores. We'd love to have you join us," he said. Then he realized the one flaw in the plan. "That is, if you can take off on a weekend."

Colby bit the corner of her pouty lip. "Normally, I can't," she admitted. "Fridays and Saturdays are super busy at the restaurant, at *any* restaurant really. The earliest I'd usually get off is eight, and that's rare. But I guess family businesses do have some perks..." She tilted her head and thought for a moment, then smiled at Emma. "Golden birthday, huh? The big one-two?"

Emma nodded. "Only one year left before I'm officially a teenager."

"And Dad officially has a coronary," Colby added with

a grin. She slid her phone out of her pocket and her fingers began flying across the screen. "Man, I haven't taken a weekend shift off in years."

His precocious daughter sent him a private wink. He knew she was playing matchmaker. Between her and Sherry, they'd have him married to Colby by Labor Day. And therein lay the problem, since by her own admitted timetable, Colby would have already returned to Vegas by then. Maybe asking her to come with them wasn't such a good idea after all.

But before he could say so, Colby lifted her head. "Rhonda says she can handle the shifts on her own." She leaned up to pocket the phone and tousled Emma's hair. She slid Jason a smile. "Any chance your tent has room for three?"

Chapter Six

Jason set down the last of the camping equipment and took a deep breath, inhaling the scent of fresh pine, wet mud, and wood smoke. Across the campground, metal clanged near the horseshoe pit. And near the edge of the bayou, standing beside her idol, Emma plunged her hand into a bag of stale bread and chucked a handful of torn pieces into the water. Mayhem instantly ensued. Dozens of paddling ducks honked and fought, diving for the same soggy piece, as birds flew from the trees, squawking their disapproval. Colby bent her head close to his daughter's ear. Emma's ponytail bounced with her laughter. And Jason's chest constricted.

How different would it be if Ashleigh were here today?

Listening to his daughter's animated laughter and glancing at the array of supplies at his feet, Jason figured probably not much. Ashleigh had been a girly-girl—she didn't *do* camping. But for Emma, he knew she would've done anything to make this the best camping trip a soon-to-be twelve-year-old could have. The same thing he and Colby were trying to do. Which led to the question he really wanted answered: what would Ashleigh think of Colby?

His wife had died way too young. They never thought to talk about the future or what they should do if tragedy struck. In Hollywood, dying heroes and heroines always encourage left-behind spouses to find love again, but Jason didn't want love. He'd been there, done that, and had the deep gash in his heart to prove it. But would Ashleigh have wanted him to remarry for Emma? Honestly, he didn't think he was selfless enough to *want* another man to raise his daughter, to have her call someone else Dad. But without a doubt, he'd want Emma to have the best life possible. If Ashleigh felt as he did — that having a two-parent household would ensure Emma's happiness — then she'd have had his blessing. Jason believed he had Ashleigh's. But Colby was not the woman for the job.

That became obvious at dinner three days ago. She was leaving at the end of summer. No amount of wishful thinking on his part would change that. He had to get back out there and start dating again. But for the last few days, he saw smoky gray eyes everywhere he looked.

Jason shook his head. He needed to keep his focus on Emma. This was her day. That's why Colby was there, not for him. With that thought firmly in mind, he squatted down and began putting up the familiar red tent.

When he and Cane had been in Cub Scouts, they'd spent a week each summer at Camp LeBeaux, learning about knots, compasses, and canoeing. Young Jason had putting up this thing down to a science, able to assemble his tent before anyone else in the troop — an important achievement when you're a growing boy and the reward was an extra hot dog. Later when he was a teenager, he and Cane's trips morphed into ones with smuggled alcohol and an excess of bad choices. But the big red tent always remained.

Except now that he had it put together, it wasn't quite as big as Jason remembered. It wasn't a pup tent or anything. It would've been fine had it just been him and Emma sleeping inside. But it wasn't anymore. Now Colby would be sharing the small space, making it smell like that floral perfume of hers. Filling it at night with her soft sighs. And lying an arm's reach away.

Jason groaned. It was going to be a long night.

Bending down, he took Emma's body pillow and shoved it right in the middle. His daughter would make an excellent buffer.

A mosquito buzzed near his ear and he slapped it. How did he get himself into this again? Oh, right, Emma. She was worth the midnight dip into the bayou he'd have to take to cool his raging libido. He was just glad he didn't have to work tomorrow. An exhausted firefighter was no good to anyone, and he sure as hell wouldn't be getting any sleep.

"Cool, you got it set up!"

Jason turned back to the water, where Emma broke into a sprint, having spotted the assembled tent. Colby strolled behind her, content to take her time. She offered him a smile and shoved her hands in the back pockets of her jeans, probably not realizing how the action made her shirt stretch across her breasts. He let his eyes linger for a moment, then looked away.

After grabbing an armful of her stuff, Emma slipped inside and began decorating the tent with the insane amount of pillows, blankets, and magazines she'd brought with her. When he'd noticed this morning how much stuff she was bringing, he almost told her it was ridiculous. The trip was for twenty-four hours, not twenty-four *days*. But he'd held his tongue. Ashleigh had been into the frilly stuff, but he'd never taken her camping. Maybe this was normal. Girls were different, he was learning. He cast a glance at his small duffel and basic sleeping bag. Very different.

"It's ah, a little cozier than I'd thought it would be," Colby said, sliding up beside him. He caught a whiff of her perfume and his teeth clenched. "Are you sure I'm not in the way here?"

"Not at all," he said, even as he watched Emma pull out more of her stuff and the limited available space inside shrink. Then he realized *where* she was putting it all. "Hey, Bug, don't you want to sleep in the middle of the tent? You know, between Colby and me? That way you can be by both of us."

Emma stuck her head out of the entrance, looked at him strangely, and then shrugged. "Not really. I like the edge. Plus, I can shove more stuff in the corners," she added, pulling out a flashlight, a stack of books, and a torn-out poster of Justin Bieber.

Jason couldn't help it. He called out, "Honey, you do realize we're only here for one night, right?"

She scrunched her nose. "Of course."

"I was just checking."

Colby chuckled under her breath. "It's a woman's prerogative to pack a ton of crap," she said with a grin when Emma resumed her unpacking. "It's important that you learn this now."

He smiled and held his palms up. "Hey, it's her weekend. I was just making a casual observation."

"You'll be happy to note that *I*, on the other hand, reined in my natural female tendencies and kept it to a change of clothes, two pairs of shoes, and a paperback."

Jason was tempted to ask what she could possibly need the other pair of shoes for, but he didn't. Again, he was learning. "Well as camp leader for this excursion, I appreciate your restraint."

"You should. It wasn't easy leaving behind my hair dryer, iPad, and NSYNC poster." She heaved a dramatic sigh and kicked a fallen pinecone with the side of her sneaker. It skittered across the uneven ground.

Without thinking he replied, "I'm sure I can think of something to make up for your sacrifice."

What the hell am I doing?

Colby's gaze jerked to his. "Like an extra s'more?"

Her cheeks colored a soft pink, hinting that another possibility had crossed her mind. One that he'd much rather explore, disapproving best friends be damned. Which of course had *him* imagining a few choice options. Such as putting the flat surface of the nearby picnic table to good use.

"If that's all the lady wants."

Her eyes fell to his mouth. What he wouldn't give to know what was going on inside that gorgeous head of hers. After a charged moment, she gave a nervous laugh. "The lady does love her chocolate." Then, blowing out a breath, she ran her hands along the sides of her jeans and bent forward to peek inside the tent. The hem of her dark blue top slid up the smooth skin of her lower back. "Looks like we'll be getting to know each other a whole lot better."

"Huh?" he asked, mesmerized by that lickable strip of bare skin.

Colby stood and nodded toward the tent. "The sleeping arrangements? We're practically gonna be on top of each other."

Jason stared down at her and barely held back a groan. That was one tantalizing image his overactive mind really did not need.

Colby, apparently realizing how her words sounded, or maybe just seeing the pained look on his face, widened her eyes. "I mean, not in a *bad* way." The soft pink of her cheeks turned a bright crimson. "N-not to say that being on top of you would be bad, either. Because it wouldn't. I'm sure it would be fine. *More* than fine."

She placed her hand on his arm then jerked it back as if burned. He glanced where her hand had been, still feeling the brush of her fingertips.

"But that's just not what I meant," she continued, needlessly. "Obviously." Closing her eyes, she sighed. Head lowered and shoulders drooping she blurted, "I promise I don't snore."

Jason laughed at the attempt at misdirection. "Good to know. I do. Like a loud chainsaw right in your ear."

She lifted her head and after seeing his teasing smile, gave him a sweet one of her own. The tightness in his chest from earlier eased. Their gazes held.

Knowing that he shouldn't but doing it anyway, Jason bent his head and whispered, "Just so we're clear, being on top of me? It would definitely be better than fine."

Colby's breath caught audibly. Jason leaned back. It had been a stupid impulse. But as he watched the blush work its way up her slender throat, and saw hunger darken those smoky eyes as they lowered to his mouth again, he was very glad he'd acted on it.

The early-May Louisiana heat shot up another notch. Colby's tongue flicked across her lips, the same lips he'd wanted to taste since they were both here a week before. He swallowed. She inched closer.

"Done!" Emma declared, crawling out from the opening of the tent.

Shit. Colby's eyes shot to his, just as shocked as he was. How could he have forgotten that they weren't alone? This woman was like his kryptonite. Colby sprung back a few steps, and Jason buried his hands in his pockets, quickly adjusting himself within his jeans.

Emma scrunched her nose at the apparent tension. She

tilted her head and shifted her gaze between them. Then, she grinned. "Is it lunch time yet?"

• • •

Approximately nine and a half hours, ten hot dogs, eight s'mores, a six-pack of Coke, and a chocolate frosted birthday cake later, Emma was asleep. How she managed the feat with that much sugar in her system was anybody's guess, but Jason's daughter was out like a light.

Leaving Colby all alone with the girl's extremely attractive father.

The attractive father who was currently stooped in front of her, stirring the charred pieces of wood in the heart of the blazing campfire. Moonlight filtered through the lattice of branches overhead, causing shadows to dance across the rippling muscles in his back.

"I don't know about you," he said, pushing to his feet. The hem of his pajama bottoms brushed against pine needles as he walked past her on his way to the big blue cooler. "But I can use a beer. Do you want one, or maybe a daiquiri?"

"Daiquiri please," she answered, wetting her lips as if she could already taste the orange-flavored Dreamsicle they'd picked up on the way to the park. That was definitely one thing her hometown got right—drive-thru daiquiri and liquor stores.

As Jason dug in the cooler for their drinks, Colby sprawled out on the black and gold lawn chairs he'd set up, letting the warm breeze kiss the exposed skin of her legs. With the sun down and her favorite cotton T-shirt and shorts pajama set on, the temperature was almost bearable. Her eyelids lowered as she listened to the creak of the branches, the crackle and pop of the fire, and the rustle of leaves under Jason's feet.

Today had been fun. She'd expected there to be awkwardness, considering she was the odd person out, but it never felt like that. If anything, she fit into their family unit almost *too* easily—something she was trying hard not to freak about. Jason and Emma had included her in everything, explaining their inside jokes and sayings, asking her questions, and showing infinite patience with her decidedly poor horseshoe skills. The sexual tension of earlier wasn't forgotten—more like kept on a warm simmer with the looks Jason sent her and his frequent excuses to touch her. But Emma never seemed to notice it and they never acted on it.

But now they were alone.

Colby had never considered the scent of Citronella and bug spray to be an aphrodisiac before, but the way her pulse was racing and her skin was tingling, she may have a new product on her hands. She felt itchy, jumpy. Both eager to see if Jason would make a move and scared that he would. What would it mean if he did? Could he really be interested in a no-strings-attached fling? And if he was, could they keep Emma from getting hurt?

None of these questions needed to be answered tonight— it wasn't as if she would sneak off and have her wicked way with him in the woods, while his daughter lay sleeping a few feet away. Just the thought had Colby swiping at imagined burrs buried in her flesh. And she didn't even want to think of the interesting places she'd find mosquito bites come morning. But it was obvious that the attraction between them was mutual. Grownup Jason was *finally* noticing her the way she'd always wanted. And they were both consenting adults. Maybe before Colby had to return to her life in Vegas, she could live out a romantic fantasy with her childhood crush.

"Here you go, one large Dreamsicle." Jason handed her a large plastic cup filled to the top with the sugary treat. If she didn't know any better, she'd think the man was trying to get her drunk. With a grateful smile, Colby wrapped her lips around the straw and pulled a large gulp of the icy liquid down her throat.

Cold.

With a shiver, she pried her mouth open and formed an *O* with her lips, dragging in warm air in an attempt to thaw out her frozen throat. "Wow that's cold," she managed to say, still sucking down air.

"Yeah, see, that's the thing about daiquiris…"

Colby threw her arm out and slapped his hard stomach. After another deep inhale, she was able to swallow a little more comfortably and she lifted her drink again. This time, taking a more controlled sip. Much better.

"I appreciate you coming today," Jason told her, eyes trained on the flickering flames. "Emma hasn't had the easiest childhood. I think we've made a good life for ourselves, but it didn't come without its share of bumps. I needed to make this day special for her. She looks up to you, and it meant a lot that you were here." He glanced over. "To the both of us."

Vulnerability and a touch of something else she couldn't decipher in the firelight sparked in his eyes. Colby swallowed. She'd never been a role model before; she doubted she was cut out for the job. And as for being motherly, she didn't know the first thing about that mess. But Emma was a great kid. "There's nowhere else I'd rather be."

They fell into silence, listening to the bustling noise of not so distant traffic on the main highway. But here, in the dark, they felt isolated. Safe. And with the daiquiri beginning to work its magic in Colby's veins, she found the courage to say, "Jason, I've been wondering about Emma's mom." What she did *not* feel brave enough to do was say Ashleigh's name aloud.

His bouncing knee stilled. "What about her?"

"Mostly about how she died," she admitted. "But if that's too painful to talk about, I totally understand."

Jason shifted in his seat. Colby waited, scared she'd pushed him too far or too soon, as he took a pull off his beer. But then he said, "No, I can talk about it. It'll always be painful, but you deserve to know." He paused to take another sip and Colby leaned closer, her own drink in her hand, anxious and a little frightened to put the final pieces into place.

"As you know, I met Ashleigh in high school," he finally said, his deep voice low and hollow. "People say you're supposed to date around, sow your oats when you're young. But I never wanted or needed to. Ashleigh made me happy. And I like to think I made *her* happy."

Jason took another sip, and Colby kept herself from interrupting. She had no doubt Ashleigh had been the happiest woman on earth. Even in high school, there was no mistaking that look of love in her eyes. You couldn't fake a look like that. And a love that inspires it doesn't fade.

"Anyway, Ash came to Ruston with me and your brother for college. Cane of course loved that—no competition for women, and I was his constant wingman." She heard the small smile in his voice as he stood, his chair creaking in the quiet. He tossed his empty bottle in the provided trashcan and grabbed another longneck from the cooler. "A few months into our junior year, Ash found out she was pregnant. We were in love, and I knew that she was it for me, so I asked her to marry me."

"I must have just left," Colby said, wondering if she would have gone to the ceremony had she stayed.

Could she have watched the crush of her life marry the love of his?

Jason nodded. "By that time I'd already gotten my Paramedics degree and I'd always planned to join the department like Dad. So we came back here."

As he took another long gulp of liquid courage, Colby studied his profile. The strong jawline and rigid set of his mouth, the tension in his shoulders. It was obvious this was difficult for him to talk about, so she gently asked, "And Ashleigh?"

With an exhale, Jason picked up the cooler, brought it with him, and then lowered himself onto the lawn chair again. "She became a paramedic, too. A good one. She couldn't deal with bugs and dirt, but blood and guts she could handle. She had the biggest heart of anyone I knew," he said, pride evident in his voice. "It's what I loved most about her."

It was strange. For years Ashleigh was around—she even came to Colby's house a few times with Jason—but Colby never knew her. Not beyond her being Jason's girlfriend. But hearing him talk about her like this made Ashleigh become real. Human. Someone other than the girl who won Jason's heart. The irrational jealousy Colby had battled all her life started to fade.

When Jason continued, his voice was almost robotic. "One night, around midnight, Ashleigh responded to a call. Chest pains. A routine situation, calls like that came in all the time. But from what the other EMTs told me, they knew something was off the second they arrived."

Colby knew how the story ended and a sense of dread curdled in her stomach. Ashleigh had been a hero. She put her life on the line for other people. The bravest act Colby had committed lately was agreeing to let Sherry give her a makeover. Nails embedding in the soft Styrofoam of her daiquiri cup, she took another sip.

"The guy was high as a kite," Jason said. "The house reeked of an intense chemical smell. And drug paraphernalia littered the floor. Rick told me they tried getting Ashleigh to head back to the truck—he had a bad feeling, and she was the only woman on the call. But she refused. She was as tough as they were, she told them, and she was there to do a job. She stooped beside the man to treat him, and that's when everything went to hell. He became violent. He cursed and spat on them, and then ran from the room. The guy's girlfriend was there—she was the one who'd made the call. And when he ran, it snapped her out of her drugged haze long enough to mention he kept weapons in the house. Ash and the guys got their shit together as fast as they could, but it wasn't fast enough. Halfway to the truck, two shots rang out. When Rick glanced back, Ashleigh was on the ground."

Jason paused to draw a breath. Voice shaking with emotion he said, "The bastard shot her in the back."

Horror swept over her. "But she was there to help him!"

Jason huffed in reply. Then he took another long gulp.

Chapter Seven

It wasn't the first time Jason had told the story. Over the years, he'd had to share it with more people than he could count. Family and friends and insurance adjusters. Emma's principal and the mailman. And about once every few months, the students in his tactical ninjitsu classes. He'd thrown himself into the sport after Ashleigh died, quickly rising to the level of instructor. During his class's sessions, Jason made sure to teach his students to be aware of their surroundings and to be prepared to defend themselves — and their loved ones — by *any* means necessary.

Weakness and vulnerability in battle, he would tell his students, whether it's in the field or in a bar room, can and often does lead to devastating consequences. It's not that his wife had been a weak person; Ashleigh probably could've kicked the shit out of several guys he knew. But she let her kind heart put her in danger. She let her guard down. And the consequence of that choice was something he and their daughter lived with every day.

"Oh, Jason," Colby said, her soft voice full of compassion. Her chair creaked as she leaned forward, closer to him. "I don't even know what to say."

Jason shook his head. "You don't have to say anything." He'd heard it all before anyway. And the genuine compassion she had shown while he told the story meant more than any empty words she could've offered.

The topic of his wife's death was heavier than he'd intended for tonight. Jason had thought they'd sit by the fire, stare up at the stars through the breaks in the trees, and pretend the air between them wasn't practically crackling with suppressed sexual tension. But when Colby asked to hear what had happened to Ashleigh, he realized he wanted her to know. He needed her to understand why he couldn't risk his heart again.

Leaning back in his chair, the weight of the story off his shoulders, Jason took another sip of his beer. A welcome buzz swam in his blood. His plan for the evening had already traveled off the expected course. So as long as they were sharing, he had a question of his own.

"You've heard my sad tale," he said, watching her closely. "Now it's your turn."

Colby choked on a mouthful of daiquiri and cleared her throat. "I don't have one."

"Bullshit." She gasped and Jason stood, planting his feet on the pine needles covering the ground. He turned his chair to face hers. Embers crackled and popped in the forgotten fire. "You don't think I remember how you used to be constantly glued to your father's side? I even remember the first batch of gumbo you made by yourself—I remember it because you were nine, and I was forced to pretend I enjoyed eating burned roux."

Colby laughed at that, and he smiled. Her lyrical laugh had that effect on him. The truth was that most of his memories of Colby as a child or a teen placed her right there in the family's kitchen with Mr. Robicheaux. Holding court over a simmering pot of okra.

"So, what?" he asked, resting his elbows on his knees. "Am I supposed to forget all that and believe you just woke up one day and decided to move halfway across the country on a whim?"

Shadows danced across Colby's face, but he saw the registered shock. "Cane and Sherry never questioned my choice."

He noted her defensiveness and nodded. "I know. When you left for New York, Cane told me it made sense. 'It's a great school and an awesome opportunity,' he'd said. And when you stayed away, moved to Vegas, and opened an *Italian* restaurant, he said it was you 'stretching your wings.' But I never bought it. Something happened, and I've always wondered what."

Colby's beautiful face clouded over and he saw the battle within. Reaching over, he opened the cooler and held up the gallon of Dreamsicle. The intention was clear; he'd shared a personal story, the hardest one he knew, and he did it fueled by alcohol. Now he was challenging her to do the same. To trust him enough with whatever it was that had chased her away all those years ago. And if needed, to rely on inebriation to do it.

She looked him in the eyes and held out her cup. "Freshman year, I was going out with this guy named Steven."

Jason nodded in encouragement as he poured.

"He wasn't the first guy I ever dated or anything. But it was my first *real* relationship, you know? My first so-called *love.*"

The sardonic twist Colby added to the word was his first sign that her story was big. That her experience had changed her. The girl he remembered had stars in her eyes and her heart on her sleeve. But with just one word, Jason realized that girl was gone. And suddenly, he had the overwhelming urge to protect the woman she'd become. To pick her up and hold her in his lap, and run his fingers through her hair as she told him whatever it was that had scarred her so deeply.

The long-buried desire, to hold and protect a woman as if she were his own, hit him like a truck. His hand wobbled while pouring her drink.

It had to be the alcohol clouding his brain. His heart knew the score.

With less than nimble fingers, Jason held out the cup and brushed hers as she accepted it. Their eyes met. And Colby released a shaky breath.

"It was the end of the semester," she continued. "I'd gotten out of an exam early and I hadn't seen Steven in a few days, so I decided to drive across campus to surprise him. I still had the extra key he'd given me the weekend before—when I'd stupidly offered to clean up for one of his frat parties." She tossed her head back and laughed. But this time, the sound wasn't musical; it was full of pain. Jason's hands fisted in his lap as she tucked her hair behind her ears. "God, I was such a sucker."

Lifting the straw to her mouth, she took a long gulp. And as Jason watched her, he decided he would very much like to meet this Steven. Preferably in a dark alley somewhere.

"So as I'm sure you've guessed by now, the real surprise was on me. There I stood in his doorway, my stupid heart full of lovey-dovey thoughts, and there he was, doing some sorority girl on the sofa. Apparently, they were so hot for each other they couldn't wait the ten steps it would've taken to get to his freaking bedroom." She blew out a breath and stared into her cup. "I took off and didn't even think about going back to the dorm. I tore out of the parking lot and headed straight for home. To *Daddy*. Because he was my hero, and he would make it all better."

Colby's voice broke on the last word, and the anger firing in Jason's gut churned, sensing how her story ended. He'd heard the rumors about her dad growing up. That was one of the things about a small town; everyone was in everyone else's business. Nothing was sacred. And very little stayed secret for long. He never knew how much the family heard because as an honorary Robicheaux, Jason hadn't talked about it. He hadn't wanted to believe that the rumors about his best friend's dad, his secondary father, and their town's former librarian were true.

"Infidelity must've been the theme of the day in my horoscope," she said, the word ending on a sob. Her chin trembled and she drew her legs up on the chair, encircling them with her arms. "At least the two of them made it to the restaurant's back office."

Jason couldn't take it anymore. He stood, set his beer down, and grabbed her hands. Colby's glistening eyes stared at him in question as he scraped the side of his boot along the ground, clearing it of any rocks and debris. Then he tugged her up.

One tear fell, and then another, as she stood on shaky legs. The sight was pure torture. He set her down on the ground and then sat as close as he could behind her, wrapping his arms around her small waist.

Gently rocking her back and forth, he asked, "Did you ever tell anyone what you saw?" He gathered her thick hair and slid it to the other shoulder. Colby slowly shook her head. "So your mom never found out?"

Colby laid her head back against his chest and gave a watery sigh. "What was I supposed to say? I didn't want to know that kind of secret. And I damn sure didn't want to share it! Mom would've been devastated."

Her shoulders shook and he tightened his grip around

her. Their mom had been the most soft-spoken, kind-hearted woman he had ever known. She'd attended daily mass and volunteered at just about every charitable organization Magnolia Springs had to offer. Colby was right; it would've devastated the woman. He couldn't imagine what it must've been like for Colby to know that kind of a secret. Or to have to keep it to herself.

"And it's not like I could tell anyone else," Colby continued. "Cane was off at school. Sherry was still a freaking kid." She huffed. "So was I. I should have never had to be in that position."

"No you shouldn't." She made a strangled sound and he smoothed a hand down her hair. "And that's why you left."

Sniffing, she bobbed her head, confirming what he already knew.

"And the aversion to Cajun food?"

Colby's trembling shoulders stilled, and she twisted in his arms. Sliding her long bare legs around his hips, her tear-filled gray eyes met his. "How did you know about that?"

Jason temporarily lost the power of speech, distracted by the sight and feel of her legs around him. His heart pounded as all his blood headed south. His pajama bottoms grew uncomfortably tight. Adjusting his hold, Jason slid his hands around her waist and the tips of his fingers slipped beneath the hem of Colby's thin cotton top.

She raised an eyebrow, waiting for an answer. The blaze of the fire at his back illuminated the splotches on her beautiful, fair face. Jason swallowed, trying to ignore the feel of petal soft skin beneath his hands. This was not the time for him to lose his self-control. Colby didn't need lust right now; she needed comfort.

"At Taste the Heat you hardly ate anything," he told her, distracted by the way she worried her lip between her teeth.

Colby's nose wrinkled as she drew a trembling breath, and he realized he'd just admitted how closely he had watched her that day. He shrugged and slid a lock of hair behind her ear. "You would only try enough to tell if the dish truly sucked or not. I've also heard grumblings about new items being added to the restaurant's menu. *Italian* ones," he emphasized, pretending to shudder. Despite her struggle to rein in her tears, Colby gave him a small, brave smile. A pang rippled through Jason's chest. "Plus the fact there isn't a Robicheaux's Two in Vegas, I took an educated guess."

She licked her lips and then rubbed them together, nodding slowly. She lowered her eyes to his chest, and her slim shoulders rose and fell with increasingly ragged breaths. Jason watched, paralyzed, as the dam of tears she'd valiantly tried to hold back, broke. "It just hurts too much."

Jason pulled her flush against him, crushing her to his chest. He cupped her head as Colby buried her face between his neck and shoulder, sobs coming freely now. She sniffled and used his shirt as a tissue, and he held her tighter, massaging her head as she cried. Letting her know he was there.

"It's okay," he whispered over and over as her breaths grew progressively jagged. He wished he could take the pain away. That he could hold her close enough that nothing could ever touch her. Tangling his fingers in her hair, he rested his forehead against hers.

In the still moments that followed, two things became clear. The first was that Jason would do anything to keep Colby from feeling this level of hurt again. A fierce need to protect was surging in his veins. And second, Jason realized the girl he once knew no longer existed. Adult Colby didn't live with her heart on her sleeve. From what she'd shared tonight, she guarded her heart almost as fiercely as he did. The two of them had a history and an unmistakable attraction. Maybe

Jason didn't have to try so hard to fight it.

Colby's shoulders shuddered with an attempt at a calming breath. Jason squeezed her tighter, stifling a groan as the tips of her breasts pressed firmly against his chest. He slid his hands to her waist, and Colby lifted her head with a shy smile.

"Feel better?"

She nodded and licked her lips. "Thank you. I don't normally do the ugly cry. It felt good." She gave a self-deprecating laugh and covered her face. "Although I'm sure I look like a hot mess right now."

Sweeping her hands aside, he glided his thumbs across her cheeks. Wiping away the lines of smeared makeup, he looked into her clearing gray eyes and said, "You're gorgeous."

A flash of uncertainty crossed Colby's face, and he bent his head to prove it.

The first brush of his lips was light. He didn't want to take advantage of her emotions. He just wanted to assure her that regardless of her tears, she was still one of the most beautiful women he had ever seen. But when a sigh escaped her parted lips, and she fisted her fingers in his hair, Jason abandoned timid and gentle. He gave in to the desire that had been snapping and building between them since the day of the competition, and proceeded to kiss her senseless.

Reaching down, he palmed the smooth skin of her calf. It felt like silk in his hands. He skimmed his fingers down the soft length to her ankle, hooking it around his hip. Colby made a satisfied noise in her throat. She wiggled closer and, happy to oblige, he tugged her fully against him and deepened the kiss. He swallowed her moan.

Leaves rustled in the wind. Unseen wings fluttered and buzzed. And their heavy breaths filled the air, turning Jason on even more. Colby's mouth tasted of citrus. Sweet, like the daiquiri she had drank, and like her. He teased the corners of her mouth. Licked the satiny skin of her upper lip. And gently bit down on her pouty lower one. He knew he needed to break the kiss soon—his daughter was sleeping in the tent only a few yards away—but this woman was like a drug. And he was quickly becoming an addict. Jason shifted to press his lips to the sensitive skin just under her ear.

Breathless and panting, Colby tilted her head as he trailed his mouth along the column of her neck. "I've always wondered," she admitted with a shiver, "what it would be like to kiss you."

He arched an eyebrow in surprise and grinned against her skin. "If memory serves me right, this is our *second* kiss."

A shocked gasp of air escaped her throat. "You remember Kiss and Catch?"

He looked at her and nodded, remembering every stolen moment of that childhood kiss.

She gazed back with dazed eyes, and chewing the corner of a slightly swollen lip, admitted, "That was my first kiss." Her tone was almost bashful, the flush of her skin darkening to rose before a hint of the vixen came back and she said, "Okay, so I've been curious how the *adult* Jason would compare."

He chuckled as he dipped his tongue into the hollow where her pulse fluttered. "And the verdict?"

"Meh."

At her laugh, which he noted sounded like music again, Jason nipped the delicate skin and then licked it. Inclining his head, he confessed, "You were my first kiss, too."

Colby went motionless in his arms and he leaned back, not surprised to see disbelief in her eyes. He shrugged. "I hadn't come out of my shell yet."

She grinned in delight.

Jason shifted her so she was out of the shadow and firelight warmed her face, then he said, "I have an idea."

"Hmm, sounds dangerous," she teased. "Any chance it involves burrs in delicate places and unexplainable mosquito bites?"

"No," he said with a laugh. "But I like where your mind is." Colby sighed with mock disappointment, and he added, "And you're not too far off."

That got her attention. Placing her hands on his thighs, she propped herself up and tilted her head, waiting for him to continue.

"Tonight I realized that we're not that different," Jason began. "We've both been burned by love, and neither of us have any interest in going back in for a round two. But we're human. We have needs. And crazy chemistry." Colby's grin stretched into a wicked smile. "What would you say to an arrangement?" he asked. "One where it's understood that feelings are off the table. Just fun, companionship, and a whole lot more of this." He grasped her hips and tugged her closer so there was no mistaking what he meant.

She shook her head with a smile but locked her ankles around his back. "You had me at crazy chemistry," she teased. Then her smile faltered a shade and she reminded him, "I'm leaving at the end of the summer."

"I know." He lifted his shoulder in a show of indifference. "It'll be a summer fling."

Colby's eyes lit up at the word *fling*. "That, sir, may just be the best idea I've ever heard." Smashing her mouth against his, she sealed their agreement with a kiss.

Victory tasted like citrus. He did it. He bought himself an entire summer with Colby, and maybe, just maybe, it would convince her to stay. He could be very persuasive when he needed to be.

And if his best friend ever found out what he just did, Jason would have his ass kicked.

Chapter Eight

Jason slid into his usual booth at Grits & Stuff, his gut a knot of twisted energy. The *clink* and *clatter* of cutlery all around him didn't help. Cane had called this afternoon, asking to meet. After the look in his best friend's eyes when Jason had suggested that very thing earlier in the week, he was justifiably cautious, and with the summer agreement he'd struck with Colby still fresh in his ears, more than a little concerned. Thankfully, he and Colby had agreed to delay their official kickoff for a time when his preteen daughter *wasn't* within listening distance, or his concern with meeting her brother tonight would be in full-out panic mode.

At the table along the far wall sat the teacher Jason had met doing a safety presentation at the elementary school last week. Across the scuffed tile floor, one of his students from the gym lifted his hand in greeting. He knew or recognized most of the patrons in the cramped café, and the majority of the remaining tables were filled—not that surprising, even despite the after dinner hour, when it was a Sunday night and the only other restaurant in town closed at eight.

The manager of *that* establishment plopped a few quarters

into the retro-style jukebox in the corner of the room and then slipped into the bench seat across from him, nodding to the server who dropped off two waters and menus. Admittedly, the all-night café wasn't the best place to have a discussion. It was loud, chaotic, and smelled faintly of a dirty dishcloth. But it would have to do. Jason was about to go on a twenty-four-hour shift and he couldn't wait that long to find out what was on Cane's mind. Or to see if the town's rumor mill had worked against him.

"How's my favorite godchild doing?" Cane asked, picking up one of the peeling menus.

Why he bothered reading it was anybody's guess because Cane always ordered the same thing—a tall stack of pancakes, a glass of sweet tea, and Hank Williams on the jukebox. The man liked his structure, for everything to stay the same. He'd been that way even in the days at Little Lambs Preschool where they first met. It was one of the reasons Jason was sweating Cane's finding out about his summer relationship with Colby so much, and it was just one of many quirks that went against his friend's rebellious appearance.

Where Jason was lean, he was broad and bulky. Cane's uniform was an array of black T-shirts, dark wash jeans, and a battered black leather jacket. With his strong jawline, hair that defied grooming, and collection of tattoos, an outsider wouldn't expect that the man was turned on by numbers. Or that he balanced budgets for kicks. The fact that Cane would one day manage Robicheaux's had never been a question when they were growing up. And, after graduating with a double major in business and accounting, that's exactly what he began doing.

Under Cane's management, the restaurant thrived; well, at least it did until they unexpectedly lost their head chef. Their father had an apparent issue with delegation, and the kitchen staff Cane had been left with included a bunch of clueless line cooks, and a sous-chef who'd bailed the first week after promotion. But with Colby back where she belonged, everything would be better. For the restaurant, for the Robicheaux family, *and* for him, Jason thought, shredding the wrapper on his straw.

"Emma's good," Jason answered, straightening the matching set of salt and pepper shakers and lining them up with the ketchup. "She's ready for school to be over. Just another week and a half to go. I dropped her off at my parents' house before coming here."

Cane nodded and pursed his lips at the appetizers list. Jason drummed a beat on the Formica tabletop. Damn, he was nervous. His friend wanted to catch up—that shouldn't be cause for alarm. The chance Cane had any clue about his plans with Colby were highly unlikely. Jason was being ridiculous.

Cane craned an eyebrow, his focus shifting to shoot his friend's musical hands a pointed look, and Jason busied himself with the water-spotted silverware instead.

He couldn't remember the last time he let anxiety get to him like this. Actually, that was a lie. He knew exactly when— the day he had to tell Ashleigh's parents that she was pregnant and ask their permission to marry her. That had been some seriously scary shit. But even though her father hadn't been a chump by any means, the older man had nothing on the kind of beat down his best friend could give him if he wanted. Jason should know; he trained Cane himself at the gym.

Maybe talk of his goddaughter would soften his buddy up. "She's looking forward to her movie date with Uncle Cane," Jason said, and when Cane's mouth lifted into a smile, he couldn't help adding, "I can't believe you're taking her to see that crap."

Flipping a page in the menu, Cane shrugged his massive shoulders. "It's our birthday tradition."

"That's just your cover," he said, swiping his sweaty palms along the sides of his jeans. "The real reason you go is because you secretly read all that teen book shit."

His friend lifted the third finger on his right hand, still without looking up from his menu. Jason laughed, feeling a small part of his apprehension fade. They both knew that he was only busting Cane's balls. Over the years, especially during the last four, Jason had tried and ultimately failed to express exactly what it meant to him that his friend cared so much about Emma. That he was willing to sit through two plus hours of hormonal teen angst just to make his daughter happy.

Cane was a good honorary uncle, a great friend, and an even better brother. But it was that last one that had the muscles in Jason's legs tensed, on high alert.

Flipping the menu to the back page, Cane raised his glass of ice water. He lifted it to his lips, but before taking a sip he asked, "You about ready to man up yet?"

He asked it so casually that Jason almost missed it. But when he caught the questioning slant of his friend's eyebrows he flinched, and his knee whacked the underside of the table. Water from his own glass sloshed along the surface. "Excuse me?"

Cane swallowed the sip he'd taken and slowly lowered the unnecessary menu with a chuckle. "You do know we live in Magnolia Springs, right?" he asked. "And that I work at Robicheaux's?"

Shit. He knew. Or at least had his suspicions. Jason shouldn't be surprised. Before he knew who Colby was, he'd flirted with her in front of the whole damn town. And Sherry was his other sister; if Cane *had* avoided the rumors from that day, he still would have heard her romanticized theories. Jason cleared his throat, trying to think of the best way to begin, and how much to reveal, but Cane continued before he could.

"I thought I'd made my stance on this clear the other day, but I guess not. I'm in charge of payroll, Jase. I know when people trade shifts. And when that person happens to be my workaholic sister, I'm gonna look into it." He folded his thick arms on the table, flexing the ink on his bicep. "So I repeat, are you ready to man up?"

Jason felt his heart rate kick into overdrive.

Cane's question was meant to be provoking. And if the man hadn't been his best friend, it would've been an entirely different story. But Cane had every right to be on edge. Jason considered explaining that Emma had been the one to invite Colby, and that she'd only agreed because it was for his daughter's birthday, but that wouldn't exactly be the truth. Emma may've been the one to ask, but Jason had wanted Colby there just as badly. And from the way Colby had responded to their kiss last night, it was possible she'd had additional motives of her own.

"All right," Jason said, cracking his knuckles. "I admit it." He scooted to the edge of the bench, on the off chance the tables around them weren't already eavesdropping on their entire conversation. "I'm attracted to Colby."

Their server approached the table and Jason sat back in his seat. A muscle twitched in his friend's jaw. He could've waved the woman away, but he needed a moment to figure out where in the hell to go from there. Did he give Cane the full truth, or only part? Did he say it was just a summer fling, or would that just make him angrier?

Which option was the least likely to get his ass kicked?

Jason glanced up at the newly hired waitress and just managed to avoid rolling his eyes. For all the woman knew, he might as well have not even been there—her suggestive smile was solely fixated on Cane. Not that Jason was surprised. It was like this wherever they went. Women were attracted to the bad boy image his friend naturally exuded. Little did the women know that a math nerd lay hidden behind the rough exterior.

But the waitress—Mandi with an I and unsubtle innuendos—was out of luck, because all of her seductive glances were wasted. Cane never took his attention away from Jason, rattling off his usual order and handing back the menu without even breaking eye contact. With a small huff, Mandi sashayed toward the kitchen, grumbling under her breath.

The moment she was out of earshot, Jason leaned forward again. "Look, man, here's the deal. I don't *need* your permission to date Colby. We're both adults, and if we want to spend time together, there's nothing standing in our way. Not as long as Emma adores her, which you should know that she does. It was her idea for Colby to come with us on the trip."

Cane didn't so much as blink at the mention of his goddaughter. Evoking Emma's name wasn't softening the big guy as much as he'd hoped. Jason exhaled a breath. Putting it all out there, he lowered his voice and raised his chin. "Man to man, you're my best friend. You're Emma's godfather and Colby's brother. I know I don't need your blessing…" He looked at his friend of more than thirty years dead in the eyes. "But I sure as hell would like it."

The jukebox shuffled and David Allan Coe's "You Never Even Called Me by My Name" poured through the speakers. Around them, diners and friends sang along to the played-out country tune. But he and Cane remained silent, although they both knew the words—it was basic Mardi Gras karaoke.

Cane narrowed his eyes but gave no other visible reaction to Jason's announcement. And for the first time in the history of their friendship, Jason realized he had no clue what the man was thinking.

Would he actually say no? Refuse to give Jason his support? And if he did, what would Jason do then? He didn't really have a contingency plan here. Everything pretty much hinged on this conversation going the way he'd hoped.

Cane cracked his neck. Taking his elbows off the table he said, "I don't get to play the big brother card often. Colby split years ago, and Sherry goes through guys so quickly that half the time I don't hear about one until she's onto the next. But I love my sisters. And I'll come after *anyone* who hurts them."

Jason nodded, in total agreement. Sherry wasn't his biological sister but if he got wind of a guy breaking her heart, he'd take enjoyment in inflicting some pain of his own. And as for Colby, well, the heat coursing through his body at the mere thought of the sexy chef was anything but brotherly, but he did feel protective of her. Just twenty-four hours ago, he'd held her in his arms, consoling her as she'd relived her most painful memories. If Jason were ever the cause of Colby feeling like that, Cane wouldn't even have to look for him. He'd gladly offer his ass up for a smack down. He'd deserve it. "You have my word that I will never hurt her."

Cane looked at him and rubbed his hand over his face. "All right, here's the deal. You're a good guy. I couldn't ask for a better friend, and you're a great dad. You've been through hell and back but you never gave up. I admire the shit out of you. But, man, let's just be real. You're not ready to move on. You've barely looked at a chick since Ashleigh died. With Emma, you're all heart, but with women—hell even with your friends to some degree—you protect yourself. And I get it. No one should have to go through what you did. It changes you. But Jase, Colby is my sister. And friend or not, if things go bad and her heart gets broken, we *will* have a problem."

Jason had never seen that particular look in his friend's eyes before. At least not directed at him. And of course, he was right about everything. Cane wasn't known for heartfelt speeches, but when it was important, if it was something he felt strongly about, the man didn't pull any punches.

After Ashleigh died, Jason *had* changed. And if he hadn't learned that Colby was just as cautious as he was, they wouldn't even be having this conversation. He wouldn't pursue her. But that's what made them perfect for each other. Neither of them was looking for love. They'd both been there and gotten the battle scars to show for it.

"I hear what you're saying, man," Jason told him. "And you're right. But Colby told me her plans to leave at the end of the summer. We're keeping it casual, just two friends hanging out."

He picked up his water glass and drained half its contents in one gulp. He conveniently left out that if she changed her mind, and stayed in Magnolia Springs permanently, all the better. Odd that a summer of hooking up was better than the truth.

"Good." Cane shifted in his seat, stiff vinyl cracking under his weight. His thick eyebrows drew together. "Colby's trust level with men has been shot to hell. I have my suspicions as to why, but let's just say my sister doesn't believe in white picket fences anymore. I'd hate to see you or my godchild hurt expecting more."

Jason schooled his features, giving nothing away. But could he know about, or at least suspect, their father's infidelity? If not, it would do his friend no good to learn of it now. As curious as he was, Jason left the words unsaid and simply told Cane, "I know what I'm doing."

For several long moments, Cane didn't say anything, his emotionless eyes giving nothing away. Then the pensive look faded from his friend's features and Jason smiled, finally feeling like things were going his way. The coiled muscles in his neck and shoulders relaxed.

Taking a needed breath, he looked again across the crowded diner and saw a familiar redhead walk through the front entrance.

Angelle was one of the new volunteers at the station, a sweet girl who was a transplant from Cajun country. She'd only been with them for two months, but after a bit of a shaky and hesitant start, she was turning out to show impressive determination. Her deep-set eyes scanned the crowded café and when they landed on Jason's booth, they widened in delight.

"Who is that?" Cane asked, craning his neck around to see what held Jason's attention.

"A new recruit at the station." Casual or not, the last thing Jason wanted was for his friend to think he was messing around behind Colby's back. "Angelle's just a friend."

"That's good to know." Cane's head tilted as he watched Angelle maneuver her way around the crammed tables and chairs, needless apologies falling out of her mouth. Her purse strap caught on a man's chair and yanked her back after a few steps. Jason could hear the grin in his buddy's voice when he said, "Then introduce me to your friend."

Cane turned his body in the seat to get a better look at Angelle moving across the floor. Although Jason couldn't see his face, he knew the instant the two of them made eye contact.

It wasn't that the normal reaction flashed across the woman's pretty face; it was actually far from it. Normally, women turned into a puddle of goo whenever they set their sights on his best friend, much like Mandi did earlier. But Jason's newest volunteer shortened her steps, almost as if she were debating turning back the way that she came. The wideness of her eyes turned from one of happiness to one of apprehension, and her slim shoulders seemed to shrink into themselves. Jason couldn't help but chuckle under his breath. Apparently, there was at least one woman in town who was immune to Cane's charm.

"Hey, Angelle," he said, watching her take the last few steps as if her feet were weighted with lead. He shouldn't be so amused, but he was. "I'd like you to meet a friend of mine, Cane Robicheaux."

Cane did what he always did when he actually gave a shit about a girl; he leaned back and leisurely lifted his gaze to look in her eyes as he dropped the bomb—the slow build to a grin that unveiled his biggest asset, the dimple in his left cheek. Women swooned over it every time. But Angelle was quickly becoming Jason's favorite person in the world because she didn't let out a breathy whimper, or play with her hair. Nope, she looked like she wanted to throw up.

Jason snickered and Cane's grin dropped. This night had definitely taken a turn for the interesting.

Angelle shoved her red hair behind her ear, exposing the ink on the inside of her wrist. Cane's admiring appraisal flicked to the one-word tattoo: *Chance*. She mumbled a quick hello, then focused her attention back on Jason with a wild look in her eyes.

"I won't interrupt your dinner," she said, her words coming out unnaturally fast and tight. "I just saw your truck outside and since Rob and I traded shifts, and I knew I wouldn't see you at the station tomorrow, I wanted you to know that I've decided to join your class."

Jason blinked from the verbal explosion. It was a good thing he had years of experience deciphering fast-paced Emma-speak. "My class?" he asked. "You mean at the gym?"

She nodded. "It's tomorrow night, right?"

"Ah, well, yeah," he said, more than a little surprised. The woman had changed a lot from the meek girl he'd met a couple months ago, but enrolling in ninja-style martial arts was a bigger step than he would've expected. Angelle's hopeful smile seemed to fade at his hesitation and he quickly added, "That's great, Ang. I won't be there—I'll be on shift—but my assistant is excellent. I think you'll really enjoy it."

The full-watt smile returned, and her gaze flitted to Cane. It was so quick it was as if she did it on instinct, then she took a step closer to Jason. Lowering her voice to a throaty register she said, "If it's with you, I'm sure I will."

Now it was Jason's turn to widen his eyes. He immediately turned to Cane, lifting his palms up in a show of innocence, and found his friend studying them both with avid interest.

What the hell? In the two months he'd known the kid—hell, he guessed Angelle wasn't a kid; he was pretty sure her paperwork said she was twenty-six—she'd never once come on to him or made a flirtatious comment. The first few weeks she had barely talked at all. And he knew for damn sure he'd never made a pass at her. The woman was cute, but she wasn't his type.

So then why did she choose tonight, in front of Colby's brother of all people, to make a move?

Oblivious to his distress, Angelle shifted her shoulders back and smiled, her eyes dancing with pride like she'd just performed a dare. "I'm looking forward to sweating with you in the future," she declared before turning and promptly tripping over her own two feet.

The moment Angelle was a table length away, Jason looked at Cane and assured his friend as emphatically as he could, "Dude, I swear nothing's going on with her."

Cane didn't acknowledge him. He just turned his head

to watch the redhead weave back around the restaurant. But when she reached the door and bit her lower lip, a rare glimpse of the unsure girl Jason had met two months ago resurfacing, he heard Cane say, "I think I'm in love."

Chapter Nine

"A fling with a fireman," Colby said aloud to the empty kitchen of Robicheaux's as she formed another meatball with her gloved hands. The stainless steel range hood reflected back her giddy grin. "When exactly did my life morph into the plot of a romance novel?"

The question, of course, was rhetorical. Not only because she was alone and didn't expect the walls to answer, but also because she already knew the exact moment she transformed from a spinster chef into a thirty-year-old woman with a raging libido. It was at the campground three nights ago, when her childhood crush wiped the mascara from her eyes, pulled her into his strong arms, and kissed the ever-loving stuffing out of her.

A delicious shiver ran down Colby's spine at the memory.

Things like that, sensual and erotic encounters, didn't happen to her. Neither did agreements of friends-with-benefits. Wild affairs were her sister's domain—Colby was the cautious one. The boring one. And lately, the hard up one. She never leaped without a thorough examination and game plan (which explained why she thought of nothing else for the last seventy-two hours), and never when her heart was in danger of being put on the line. Love wasn't an option, so she steered clear of anyone who could want more than she was willing to give—or anyone who might tempt her to believe in the fairy tales she grew up reading. Staying away from the whole mess was Self-preservation 101. But when it came to Jason, Colby was discovering that her standard mode of operation no longer held as much appeal.

She reached her hand into the gleaming silver bowl and pinched off another portion of flavorful meat, tuning out the nagging voice that warned an affair with Jason wouldn't be enough. That at the end of the summer, regardless of their agreement, she'd be tempted to stay, to ask him for more. She nudged the radio with her elbow, hoping the peppy Carrie Underwood song admonishing a good girl would drown out the decidedly unhelpful thoughts.

Besides, she'd heard Jason's story. Regardless of what her long-buried, inner-romantic may lead her to want later, the man had battle scars of his own. He wasn't looking for a long-term relationship. And he knew she was jetting back to Vegas in a few months. So really, this was the closest thing to a safe scenario she could get. And the icing on the cake was that the man in question was *Jason*—the epitome of every childhood fantasy she'd ever had. If Colby *didn't* take advantage of this opportunity, she'd kick herself for the rest of her lonely, pathetic, celibate life. As it was now, she had a pretty decent hunch she was headed toward life as the eccentric cat lady, known by the neighborhood kids for her delicious hot and spicy gumbo. Gumbo she couldn't even bring herself to eat.

The only real question left in the equation was Emma. Colby wasn't stupid, or blind. She saw the way the girl watched her, saw the smiles Emma thought she hid as she blatantly played Cupid between her father and Colby. The preteen could give Sherry a run for her matchmaking dollars. And Colby totally got it. Jason was doing an amazing job, but it was natural for the girl to want a woman, a *mother* in her life—but that wasn't a role meant for her. She didn't know the first thing about raising kids, and she had no plans of changing that.

Nope, the way Colby saw it, she could only agree to a casual fling with Jason on the condition that from here on out, they kept their relationship completely platonic in front of Emma. No more camping trips or cozy dinners with just the three of them. She couldn't stomach the young girl getting her hopes up, or being the reason she was hurt again.

With a decisive nod, Colby set the last rolled meatball on the tray. Prep time always cleared her head. She covered the platter with plastic wrap and shoved it into the walk in. Then, after making sure Rhonda had everything she needed for the new menu items, she whipped off her gloves and tossed the latex in the trash. Combing through her bag, she found her favorite lotion and squirted two dollops into her cupped hands, thinking again she needed to buy stock in the stuff. One of the drawbacks of wearing gloves all day and constantly plunging your hands into hot water was skin that occasionally felt as luxurious and enticing as a rhino's butt.

As Colby massaged the soothing cocoa butter into her rough hands, the faint scent of chocolate filling her head, her mind tripped back to her fireside make-out session with Jason. And the way *his* hands had felt kneading her skin. Her legs tingled and she closed her eyes, leaning her hip against the counter.

Damn, that man could kiss. Better than any daydream she'd ever had about him, that was for sure. She opened her eyes as a slow smile crossed over her face. And now that they'd struck their agreement, hopefully she'd discover *other* things the Captain could do well, too.

An hour later, Colby pulled into the packed parking lot of Magnolia Springs Elementary. Staring up at the familiar two-story building brought back a flood of memories. Days of science fairs and field days, quiz bowls and the school paper. Colby had never really found her niche until high school where they finally had home economics—now *that*, she rocked.

She planted a black stiletto onto the steaming concrete and walked up to the entrance with purposeful strides. The *click* of her shoes on the pavement matched the rhythm of her pounding heart. She was running later than she would've liked—and she despised being late. But, as luck would have it, her unreliable car had decided today would be a great day to be difficult. That's what she got for asking her sister to have a car waiting for her when she arrived, instead of just renting one herself.

When Emma had called her the night before, inviting her to the Recognition Assembly, Colby had been conflicted. It was sweet to be included, and she wanted to be Emma's friend. But she didn't want to confuse the young girl. Would going only serve to lead her on? Events like these were for family members, not a woman about to be secretly hooking up with a student's dad. In the end, Colby knew what a big deal this assembly was within the school and the community, so she accepted. She just hoped she made the right choice.

Taking a quick moment to peer inside the glass double doors of the main building, Colby noticed that everything looked exactly as it did when she was a student there. Beige linoleum floors, light blue cinder block walls, and bright red lockers on either side of the hall. A poster declared *The Frogs Are Fierce*, because, sadly, that was the elementary school's mascot.

Beware the fearsome frogs.

Chuckling softly, she continued toward the cafegymatorium, which she had no doubt still smelled faintly of spaghetti sauce, regardless of what the staff had made for lunch. She yanked open the door and inhaled the basil. A sea of multi-colored plastic chairs stood before the makeshift stage, making the room look as if a rainbow had thrown up. Colby shook her head, a nostalgic smile tugging at her lips. Then she searched the room for Jason.

With a population of just over a thousand people, the town never felt the need to divide the students into a middle school or junior high, which meant that all the children in Magnolia Springs from preschool to preteen passed through these doors. That was a lot of families. It also meant that they were in for a long ceremony today. Colby didn't mind. Looking at the adorable faces on the stage, she couldn't help remembering all the years she'd sat up there waiting for her own awards. Searching for *her* parents watching in the crowd, proud smiles pasted on their faces.

The pang that hit Colby's heart was double-edged. The turmoil was expected; her emotions always got twisted when she remembered her dad in happier times. But now a strange ache in her chest accompanied the confusion. She would never know what it was like to sit in the rainbow throw-up chairs and smile as *her* children received an award. It was one of the consequences of giving up relationships that she rarely let herself think about. And spotting Jason in the front row, she decided today was not the day to start.

As Colby made her way toward the front of the room, sidestepping purses and protruding feet in the aisle, Jason's handsome face lit up in a welcoming smile. Fine lines around his eyes crinkled. His gaze lowered to her mouth, and that toe-curling grin turned wicked. Colby's breath faltered, and a wave of heat rushed over her.

Forget *People* magazine. Jason was hands down the sexiest man she had ever seen. Today he was dressed in pressed pants and a dark green button down, and he looked positively scrumptious. It was unfair for a man to look this good in everything he wore; there had to be a few men in town who'd appreciate him sharing the wealth. Jason's toffee eyes danced with devilish intentions, confirming the decision she made on their camping trip. Now it was only a matter of getting him alone...

She came to a stop before the open seat he had saved for her, loving the way he looked into her eyes as if he *really* saw her. He held her gaze for a long, delicious beat, then pressed a warm hand against her lower back as he turned them both to reintroduce her to his parents. A thrill skipped over her skin.

Waving away the introduction, Colby smiled at the woman seated in front of her and said, "Mrs. Landry, it's been way too long."

Her favorite teacher shot to her feet with a laugh, leaving no mistake who Emma had inherited her energy from. "Mrs. Landry is what my students call me," the woman scolded with a grin. "And seeing you all grown up and calling me that makes me feel old. Please call me Sharon."

Sharon wrapped her up in a hug, and Colby inhaled the comforting scent of Chanel No. 5 and baby powder. It transported her right back to the days of seventh grade, when life's dilemmas involved gossiping friends, passing earth science, and mastering her father's corn and crabmeat soup recipe. Oh, and the unrequited crush she'd had on her teacher's son, of course.

Jason's mom smiled. She looked around the room packed with former students, then lowering her voice conspiratorially said, "You always were one of my favorites."

Colby laughed. Sharon squeezed her hand and sat down, and Colby turned to the distinguished gentleman on the woman's left. "It's nice to see you again, Chief." The man might've retired from the fire department years ago, but in her eyes, he'd forever hold the honorary title. Jason's dad was larger than life with broad shoulders, a generous stomach, and an air that commanded your respect. "I hear you have more time for fishing these days."

"That I do," he said, pushing to his feet with a chuckle. "But the dang things still aren't biting." He leaned in to press a chaste kiss on her cheek, tickling her skin with his salt and pepper whiskers, and tilted his chin toward the stage. "Do you know that all I've heard out of my granddaughter this past week is Miss Robicheaux this, and Miss Robicheaux that? It seems as though you have yourself a fan club."

Anxiety crept back as Colby followed his smile to see Emma seated in the second to last row at the end of the stage, waving eagerly. She waved back, her chest growing uncomfortably tight, and said, "The feeling is mutual, Chief."

That's what made this so hard. Colby genuinely liked the girl. But between attending a school function, going on a family trip, and talking Emma through a monumental first like getting her period, everything was beginning to feel just so *domesticated*.

Emma lifted her palm to block her other hand and pointed at the boy beside her. "That's *him*," she mouthed, dramatically widening her eyes.

Colby laughed, knowing exactly who *he* was. During the camping trip, she'd gotten an earful about Brad, the mega-crush Emma had on him, and the fact that her dad would go positively butt-crazy—her words, obviously—if he found out that Brad had told Molly who told Ava who told Emma that he liked her. "He's cute," she mouthed, nodding her approval.

When Colby turned back, she found the Chief watching her with a strange expression on his face. Not unfriendly by any means; more like curious, appraising. Questioning. His eyes cut to Emma, and then to Jason, and the corners of his mouth twitched. Her heart rate did a funny dance. She had a feeling his parents were getting an entirely wrong picture here. The same one she feared *Emma* was getting.

Unfortunately, the principal chose that moment to walk up to the podium. "Welcome family and friends to Magnolia Springs Elementary's Recognition Assembly!"

The crowd broke into applause as Principal Levet adjusted the microphone, and Colby reluctantly took her seat between Jason and his mother. If she wasn't careful, it looked like the entire town would have the two of them engaged before they even officially sealed their little agreement. And marriage was *so* not in her future.

The cheers died down and the principal smiled. "As you all know," she said, folding her hands in front of her, "next week our students will finish up the year, taking end of term exams and participating in the school-wide field day. But today we honor them for their many extra-curricular achievements. It's no secret that MSE has some of the most active, involved students on the north shore. So parents go ahead and get comfortable"—she gave the crowd a knowing smile—"because we're gonna be here for a while."

The audience laughed in appreciation, and the woman went on about the school's award-winning choir and band. But Colby couldn't shake the look she'd caught on the Chief's face. Settling back against the stiff plastic of her chair, she gnawed on her lip.

She hadn't been overly close with either of his parents, but she'd known them all her life. Because of Cane, the Landry family became fixtures around their house early on. They came to holiday parties, tagged along during a trip to Florida one year, and they were Robicheaux's most loyal customers. His parents had always gone out of their way to make her feel comfortable, and Colby hated the thought of disappointing either of them.

This *thing* with Jason kept getting stickier and stickier, and technically it hadn't even started yet. But Colby was too far-gone to think about backing out. Even in the packed room, her entire right side tingled with awareness of the sexy captain. With the entire summer still stretched before them, all she could do was follow her heart—or in this case, hormones—and vow to keep in touch with Emma when their arrangement ended.

The choir members returned to their seats, certificates in hand, and Principal Levet reached for her bottle of water. As she uncapped the top, Emma caught Colby's eye and grimaced. Colby grinned. Emma's group must be up next.

Setting the bottle on the podium, the principal cleared her throat. "Our student council has been extra active this year," she said, confirming Colby's suspicion. "Our class presidents banded together to raise money for our tutoring program, earning enough to purchase two new computers and a slew of reference materials for the library. Emma Landry, our sixth grade president, also chaired a baked goods drive for our literacy program."

Irrational pride bloomed in Colby's chest as the row of class presidents stood to a round of applause. Emma's drive and ambition had absolutely nothing to do with her, but it didn't stop her from practically gloating on the girl's behalf. When Emma neared the front of the line to receive her certificate, Colby even joined the Landry family in catcalls. Jason let out an impressive whistle. His parents screamed her name. And Colby stamped her feet and whooped. Jason caught her eye and winked.

"Way to go Em!" Sharon cheered beside her as Emma posed for the school photographer.

"That's my peanut," the Chief called out.

Around them, people laughed good-naturedly at the attention, and Emma's face turned beet red. But from the mega-watt smile on her face, there was no mistaking that she was pleased.

Colby took in the scene with a heart split straight down the middle. It was awesome seeing Emma so happy. She was glad to be here and honored to have been asked. But the same question kept repeating in her mind: what kind of signal was she sending? To Emma, to Jason, to his parents...to herself?

Up and down, back and forth. Her emotions were like a freaking roller coaster. She wasn't a member of the Landry family, but she was for damn sure acting like she was. Colby drew a series of short breaths, suddenly feeling like she couldn't inhale any deeper.

It was too much. Too fast. She'd only been in Jason's life again for, like, two *weeks*.

What was going on with her?

By the end of the assembly, Colby had barely managed to get her breathing back under control when Emma came barreling toward them. Jason scooped her up and squeezed her tight against his side.

"I'm so proud of you," he said, mussing her hair as he jostled her back and forth. During the last hour, Emma had racked up additional certificates for library helpers, peer tutoring, and volleyball, and if Colby had to wager a guess, she'd had the loudest cheering section of any other recipient. Emma buried her face in his chest and wrapped her arms around his waist, regardless of the fact that Brad and her classmates were all around. "By the time you graduate from this place, they're not gonna know what to do without you."

Emma blushed. "I didn't really do anything that special."

"Em, your dad's right." Putting on a smile, Colby began counting on her fingers. "Chairing a bake sale, tutoring, working in the library, *leading* the volleyball team in assists— as someone who has zero coordination, let me just say that I'm very impressed."

The girl laughed, but not before beaming even brighter. Pushing her bangs out of her face, she widened her eyes and asked, "You *are* coming to eat with us at Honey and Pop's, aren't you?"

Colby scrunched her nose at the abrupt subject change, and the strange names. Jason chuckled, seeing her confusion and explained, "Honey and Pop are my parents. We're going over there for dinner. And yes, we'd really love it if you joined us."

She hesitated—which was a feat in the face of Emma's fresh-faced eagerness. But she'd been looking forward to a quiet night alone to freak out. And wouldn't tagging along lead to more of the same confusion? The deal she made with Jason wasn't about sweet family moments. It was a night between the sheets, not dinner at mom and dad's. Unless said dinner included a night of babysitting services and a green light for hooking up.

But before Colby could come up with a halfway decent excuse, Sharon squeezed her shoulder. "You know I have enough food to feed an army," she cut in with a twinkle in her eye. "And it would be an honor to serve a renowned chef. Well, as long as you don't turn into one of those judges on *Iron Chef.* Those people can be brutal."

Even the Chief jumped in, saying, "Yes, you should join us," which actually only proved her point. Colby knew what he was thinking, what he thought was happening between her and Jason.

All four of them were looking at her with such hopeful expressions that Colby couldn't help feeling a strange tug. Of belonging, of feeling as though she fit into their sweet family unit. And *wanting* to fit into it even more.

That desire scared her.

This was only a fling. It was all it could ever be. And she needed to remember that.

Then Jason tilted his head to the side and a spark entered his eye. She didn't know where it came from, didn't know what it meant, but it *felt* like a challenge. A challenge she wanted—no, needed to meet. Turning to Emma and against her own better judgment she asked, "So what's for dinner?"

• • •

"Everything all right in here, Dad?"

Jason knocked on the partially open door to his father's study. The women were huddled together in the kitchen, cooking up a storm and outnumbering him with estrogen. He prided himself on being a decent cook, but the expression "too many cooks in the kitchen" existed for a reason. So he and his Y-chromosome had left.

When his old man hadn't been glued to the television set in the living room, he'd headed here. And now that he'd found the man in his favorite hiding spot, Jason knew something was wrong.

By nature, Robert Landry was outgoing and talkative. He had a way of pulling anyone around him into a conversation, and he could go on forever about almost anything. Anything except his feelings, that is. Other than anger, emotions of any kind, in his father's opinion, were strictly women's territory. But after the assembly, he'd been uncharacteristically quiet.

"Huh?" His father spun his leather executive chair away from the window, looking up with an expression that said he'd been somewhere else entirely. "Oh, sure, sure."

Jason nodded, not for a moment believing it. Wisps of the man's hair stood on end, as if he'd raked his fingers through it without thought, and his mouth was set in an inscrutable line.

Gesturing from behind a desk cluttered with fishing knickknacks, a bowl of hard candy, and framed pictures of Emma, he said, "But close the door and sit with me for a spell, will you?"

Warily, Jason turned around and did as asked, his palm lingering on the stained wood. The last time his dad asked him to "sit for a spell," he had been nine and about to be reamed for pantsing his cousin at a crawfish boil. The same feeling he got then—and the one he still got right before he ran into a burning building—began churning in his gut. But this was why he had sought his father out. To see what was going on in that noggin of his. So he took a seat on the armrest of a wingback chair and asked again, "You sure everything's all right?"

His father nodded wordlessly, focusing on a point just above Jason's head. He pinched his pursed lips between thick fingers. The second hand on the mounted trout clock *tick*ed ten times, then in a thoughtful voice, his father broke the silence.

"I loved Ashleigh like she was my own daughter."

The muscles in Jason's back tensed. And the churning feeling in his stomach escalated. Of all the things that could've come out his old man's mouth, he never would've expected *that*.

It's not that he doubted his father's sincerity—he *had* treated Ashleigh like a daughter. But in the last four years, Jason couldn't recall a single conversation his father had initiated about her.

Where is he going with this?

His father's clear eyes met his. "She was a good woman, son. A strong woman. And this family will always miss her."

Now it was Jason's turn to nod, his throat closing like it did every time talk turned to his wife. Swallowing past the emotion, he said, "I know, Dad. And Ashleigh would've loved being there today." His lips tugged into a smile, picturing it.

His wife had been the proudest, most involved mom he'd ever seen. And that was saying a lot, since his gave the mother on *Everybody Loves Raymond* a run for her money. But from the day Emma had entered kindergarten, Ashleigh had been the class mom. She'd been the go-to helper when the teachers needed anything. A story reader, field trip chaperone, class play organizer. She'd made it a priority to enroll Emma in every activity their daughter showed a remote interest in, and she never missed a single class, game, or performance. When she died, along with leaving him with a broken heart, Ashleigh had left behind impossible shoes to fill, especially for a single parent. But Jason had done his best to fill them. And he'd done a damn good job, too.

He never missed a game or performance, either. He signed up for more than his share of field trip duty. And he even learned how to sew so he could add Emma's Girl Scout patches to her uniform. Sure, his mom could've done it, but he wanted to. He hated asking for more help than was absolutely necessary. His parents already pitched in enough, watching her during his all-day shifts, driving her to and from school, and helping with her homework. It was hard enough being a firefighter with two parents at home much less with only one, but somehow he and Emma had made it work.

But now, Jason was ready to move past simply making it work. He was finally ready to give Emma the life that a drug addict stole from her four years ago.

Suddenly eager to be back in the kitchen, cooking beside his daughter and staring into Colby's smoldering eyes, Jason stood and gestured toward the door. "Well, I just wanted to check in." He took a step in the direction of the exit. "But we have company so I guess I should—"

"Son, wait a minute."

Jason exhaled. Apparently, there was more to the man's strange mood than thoughts of Ashleigh. His father rose from the chair, his bushy eyebrows drawn together. As he walked around the desk, Jason sank into the worn out cushion of the upholstered chair. "All right, Dad. Something is obviously bothering you." He swiped a Wild Cherry Life Saver from the glass candy dish in front of him and propped his ankle on his knee, feeling like a skipping track on Emma's iPod as he asked again, "What's going on?"

Snatching a Butter Rum candy from the bowl, his father popped it into his mouth and chomped loudly, breaking it into tiny pieces as his fingers played absently with the plastic wrapper. "You know your mother worries about you," he said, dropping the bomb as if it was common knowledge. Actually, Jason hadn't known that. But he probably should have. The woman worried about everything. Then the old man scratched the side of his neck and added gruffly, "We both do."

His father coughed and looked away—but not before Jason saw the unmistakable sheen in his eyes. It would've been less jarring if the man had punched him, though the effect would feel about the same. He watched his father push to his feet and stride toward the window overlooking the backyard.

Centered in the blind-covered frame stood a large oak tree, his dad's favorite hammock swaying below it in the late spring breeze. His childhood tree house was perched high above that. Jason still remembered everything about the summer he and his dad built it. For weeks, they'd poured over design books, choosing the perfect model and then selecting just the right wood. They had gathered materials, talked strategy, and set to work putting it together. While they labored, they'd discussed "manly" things: the correct tool for the job, LSU and Saints football, girls, and even school—but never anything deeper than that. In fact, other than the time his father held his newborn granddaughter in the hospital or slapped Jason's back at Ashleigh's funeral, this was the most emotion he'd ever seen his father express.

"When you and Ashleigh first came to me, saying you wanted to get married and raise Emma, I had my concerns." He flicked a slat of the blinds, for all appearances consumed with the blades of grass in his lawn. "I knew you were doing the right thing, but in many ways you were children yourselves. A marriage needs more than just attraction. It takes commitment and love. The kind of love that can endure a hurricane and still stand come morning. To be frank, I wasn't sure the two of you had it. But you proved me wrong. That girl loved you, and I know you loved her." He released the blind caught between his fingers. "I could see it when you looked at her."

When his father turned, the cloud that had overshadowed him all afternoon lifted as a relieved smile broke across his face. "That same look was in your eyes today."

Jason's eyebrows snapped together. Of course he loved Emma. Was that supposed to be a revelation? He asked his father as much, but the old man didn't answer. He just kept watching him with a strange look of annoying, unprecedented patience. Then after a moment, the meaning behind his words finally sank in.

"Wait, you think I'm in love with *Colby*?"

His father shrugged a shoulder. A shade of uncertainty

crept into his tone as he said, "I admit I thought it was rather soon. You've only become acquainted again for a couple weeks—"

"Eleven *days*," Jason cut in.

The whiskers framing his mouth twitched. "Eleven days," he amended. "But the heart doesn't always work on a timetable. And besides, you've known Colby a long time. The two of you did grow up together."

Jason pinched the bridge of his nose, wondering what in the hell was happening. His emotion-free dad was talking about the *heart*, for God's sake. What would the old man do for an encore, quote Oprah?

Through the crack in the door, Jason could smell sautéed bell peppers and onions. He could be out there, sampling whatever it was the women were cooking, and pretending this entire conversation had never happened. His legs twitched with the desire to bolt. But he owed it to his normally tightlipped father to hear him out—even if what he was saying was completely ridiculous.

His father steepled his fingers and studied him. "Listen son, life dealt you a hell of a hand. It takes time to recover from something like that. But you deserve to be happy." His voice grew thick with meaning as he added, "And so does my granddaughter."

Of all the things he said, those words rankled. Jason shot to his feet. No shit, Emma deserved to be happy. That was why he'd started thinking about marriage again in the first place. Everything he did was for his daughter.

From his perch beside the window, his father watched silently as Jason paced the length of the room.

There was no doubt that over the last week and a half, Colby had made a difference in their lives. She'd been there during the debacle at the convenience store. She'd offered

Emma advice that no amount of book reading would've prepared Jason to give. And she'd given his daughter a much needed role model. As for him, Colby had brought him to life again. She made him laugh, turned him on, and had him feeling things he hadn't felt in years—but that didn't include love. It couldn't.

Right?

Jason shoved a hand through his hair. After Ashleigh died, his heart had closed itself off. It wasn't something he'd consciously tried to do, it just happened. Self-preservation. He assumed it would always stay that way. That he would *want* it to stay that way. But could his father be right?

Jason admired Colby. He desired her. They had a level of comfort with each other that could take him years to develop with someone else, and for the kind of marriage he wanted, there was no woman in the world who fit him better. She was great with Emma, and his daughter adored her... But did all that mean he could fall for her?

More than the voice in his head screaming *yes*, his father's reputation had him wavering. In the Magnolia Springs fire department, Robert Landry's shrewd, astute observations were stuff of legend. In an emergency or pressure situation, he'd been the guy people turned to. He was always able to size up a problem in moments and make a judgment call. And 99.9 percent of the time, those decisions had been dead on. They had saved lives. But in this case, if his father was right, all of Jason's plans were up in smoke.

During their camping trip, she'd made it more than clear that she wasn't looking for love. She didn't believe in it. If by some miracle Jason did find a way to break through Colby's barriers, and help her heal from the past, it was possible she'd consider sticking around for the future. One that could involve him and Emma. But there was no guarantee she'd ever fall for him. Or welcome him loving her…if he even did.

He came to a stop in front of his father. "You do realize people don't fall for each other at the drop of a hat, right? Not outside of Hollywood." *And especially not people like me.*

His father chuckled. "Maybe they don't." Then he placed a solid hand on Jason's shoulder and said, "But son, I saw the way you looked at her."

Chapter Ten

Colby glanced at her future conquest from the passenger side of his truck. The neon light from LeJeune's bakery illuminated Jason's abnormally rigid jaw, reminding her he'd barely said two words since they'd left his parents' house. And they hadn't really had a chance to talk much before then, either. Every time Colby had felt remotely brave enough to bring up kicking off their summer fling tonight, there had been an adolescent or parental ear around, ready to overhear her pitiful attempts at flirtation. Not exactly the start she'd envisioned for her sexy night of seduction.

But now they were alone. Thoughts of what could lie ahead sent the heat inside the already toasty truck skyrocketing. *I can do this.* So he hadn't brought it up since the night of the camping trip. She could take the bull by the horns, so to speak. Women did this sort of thing every day, right? The whole 'equal opportunity, female empowerment, we are women hear us roar' jazz. She leaned her face into the stream of cool air coming from the vent. Sadly, right now she felt less like the siren she needed to be, and closer to throwing up.

Why was she so nervous? She even had a ringing endorsement from above. When it came time for her to leave and her cute, unreliable car had sputtered, groaned, and then died a horrible death, she'd figured it *had* to be a divine blessing on her plans. The unexpected vehicular demise required Jason to bring her home after all. Granted, the nuns in Sunday school had always given the impression that booty calls were frowned upon; but perhaps, in this case, heaven had made an exception for the pathetic.

Jason drummed an erratic beat on the steering wheel, matching the thrum of her nerves. His grumpy look wasn't helping. But as her little sister always said, sometimes you have to fake it to make it. And in this case, Colby definitely wanted to *make* it. So, after another block of silence, she manned up, poured on the bravado, and asked, "You okay there, Captain?"

The brief smile he shot her was more like it. "Yeah, I'm fine."

Thank God, because the bad mood vibe so wasn't cutting it as an aphrodisiac.

Then he added, "It's just been a long day. Guess I'm more tired than I thought." And the knotted muscles in Colby's stomach clenched back up again.

An exhausted seductee didn't really scream *let's get it on*, either.

But one doesn't become the owner of a popular, thriving restaurant in Vegas by letting a little complication get in her way. Grabbing hold of her deflating hopes for the evening, Colby scooted as close to Jason as the dang seat belt would allow and called upon every ounce of dormant vixen power she had.

"You sure that's all it is?" she purred, or rather, *attempted* to purr in his ear. No one in her right mind would actually call the strange, breathy rumble that came out of her mouth a purr. *Lord, I'm bad at this.* Slipping her fingers under the collar of his dress shirt, she forged ahead. "Because you seem awfully tense, and it just so happens that I know an excellent way to release tension."

Jason laughed under his breath. "I don't doubt that for a second."

She began kneading the taut muscles of his neck and a low noise emanated from the back of his throat. He pressed into her fingers. Feeling daring, she scraped her nails across his skin and his breath hissed through his teeth. Oh yeah, Jason wanted her. A thrill ran down her spine. But before she could give herself a mental high-five or begin planning tonight's lingerie ensemble, he mumbled, "Damn, I'd love to take you up on that offer."

Colby's eager fingers stilled. That didn't sound very promising. "Why do I hear a *but* attached to that statement?"

He released a heavy breath and shot her a regretful smile. "*But,* I have to be at the station earlier than normal tomorrow. I have a pile of paperwork and back to back school tours."

The neon green numbers on the dash clicked to eleven o'clock, mocking her. There went her seduction plans. Her inner-vixen rolled her eyes and fell asleep. Could he be regretting making their arrangement? Or had it been the alcohol talking, and now he'd changed his mind?

"Another twenty-four-hour shift?" she asked, squeezing his muscles tighter.

"Twenty-four on, forty-eight off."

That explained why Emma had stayed behind at his parents' house. Colby had mistakenly assumed Jason was on the same page as to where their night was headed, but then, that would've implied a parental-approved booty call, which now that she thought about it, kinda icked her out.

"Then I guess it's probably best if you just drop me off."

She flinched as the words left her mouth. There was no way he'd missed the ring of pouting in her voice. She stole a glance out of the side of her eye and the beam of a passing car highlighted his amused smile, confirming as much.

Well that's awesome. Everyone knows there's nothing sexier than desperation.

Perhaps she should just embrace the spinster life now. Get right on the whole cat thing, buy a few dozen muumuus, and call it a night.

"*But*," Jason said, interrupting her depressing thoughts with that dreaded word again. "I was hoping that you'd have dinner with me Friday night."

Colby's spirits perked up as if they'd received a shot of B-12. It was entirely possible the man was just throwing her a bone, but it sounded as if he did want to see her. Maybe their arrangement *was* still on, and her seduction plans weren't canceled but rather momentarily delayed.

Except...

"I'd love to," she replied honestly, trying and failing to conceal her mounting frustration. "*But* weekends are crazy at the restaurant. I know I traded shifts last weekend for Emma's birthday, but I really shouldn't make a habit of it. If the head chef starts skipping out, everyone will." Pressing her thumb into a stubborn knot at the base of his neck, perhaps with a bit more force than necessary, she counter-offered with, "Sunday I get off work at five though."

He grimaced. "I'm on shift that day."

Of course he was. So much for the heavenly exception she'd thought she had. At this rate, she'd be lucky if she got laid again in this century, much less in the next few days.

Jason shook his head and the soft hairs on the back of his neck tickled her fingers. "So this is what I've been missing by not dating, huh? Coordinating work schedules, synching up calendars. It's a damn miracle anyone figures it out."

Colby's head snapped up. Color her optimistic, but that sounded like he hadn't dated anyone since Ashleigh died. But that couldn't be right. The man was sex on a stick. He was gorgeous, smart, kind, and a freaking hero in their town. Magnolia Springs didn't exactly have a huge dating pool to begin with, and a catch like Jason floating around would've been like a beacon to every single female in the Greater New Orleans area.

From their conversation the other night, Colby knew that Jason wasn't in the hunt for a relationship. But in the last four years, there had to have been at least a *few* one-night stands.

Could it be there was never anything more significant than that?

She knew it was none of her business. She wasn't in the market for a relationship either, so his dating history shouldn't matter. But suddenly it did. And she *had* to know. Telling her reasonable inner voice to stuff it, she blurted, "When was the last date you went on?"

Smooth, Colby. Real smooth.

"Last *real* date?" Jason scrunched his forehead in thought. "Junior year at LA Tech. Dinner and a poetry reading." He shot her a look. "*Totally* Ash's choice, by the way, and I blew off work to do it."

Colby's selfish heart did a tap dance. She turned to look out the window, biting off a grin. "You rebel, you."

"Reformed rebel," he corrected. "Sadly, that stuff doesn't fly when you're the captain of the fire department, owner of a gym, and the father of an impressionable girl." He paused and added, "No matter how badly I want to see the woman in question."

Colby couldn't help herself. Letting her smile fly free, she looked back at Jason and goose bumps tingled at the heat in his eyes.

"Any chance you're available Monday?" he asked, holding her gaze for a beat before returning his attention to the road.

In lieu of the exultant *whoop* she wanted to scream, Colby leaned close to Jason's ear. Brushing her lips across his skin, and grinning at his sharp intake of breath, she whispered, "I'm always off on Mondays."

"Well, hallelujah."

They both laughed as the truck rolled to a stop in Sherry's empty driveway. Monday was still five days away, but at this point, she'd take it. Besides, there was virtue in delayed gratification, wasn't there? The important thing was making sure Jason spent the time between now and then thinking about her—and how good they'd be together when the blessed night finally arrived.

Feeling emboldened by the shadows and their miraculously synched schedules, Colby unfastened her seat belt and slid across the bench seat, her linen pants whispering across the leather as she closed the sliver of distance remaining between them. "Sounds like you've got yourself a date, Captain."

Even in the dim light of the truck's cab, she could see the wickedness of Jason's grin. "I can't wait."

With a flick of his wrist, the engine fell silent. The headlights went next. They were alone, in the dark, sexual tension snapping, with no preteens sleeping nearby, and no one to interrupt. Jason tossed his seat belt and then one of them moved. She didn't know whom—didn't care, either—because then she was in his arms. On his lap. Her thighs straddling his hips, his warm hand curved around her neck, and his mouth just shy of touching hers. Right where she wanted to be.

The sound of her harsh, impatient breaths and staccato pulse pounded in her ears. Cinnamon-scented breath fanned across her skin, setting off a fire of anticipation in her blood. She swallowed, her gaze shifting between the planes of Jason's lips to the swirling desire in his caramel-colored eyes. What was he waiting for? If the man didn't kiss her soon, she was pretty sure she was going to explode.

An emotion sparked and crossed his face; it almost looked like fear. But before she could read into it or ask what it meant, his mouth came crashing down on hers. Colby sighed, her breath mixing with his. Gripping one hand around the headrest to anchor her, she slid her other down the front of his buttoned shirt and melted into his arms.

She still wasn't close enough.

Jason deepened the kiss, and she slid her arms around his waist. Dragging her nails up his back and then curling her hands around his broad shoulders, she pulled herself up hard against him, smashing her breasts into the wall of his chest. Jason growled his approval. Plundering her mouth with his lips and tongue, he inhaled her as the steering wheel dug into her back. The pale skin was going to bruise, but she didn't care. He tasted of cinnamon and temptation, and smelled like heaven.

No one had ever kissed her like this. Devoured her, as if the world could fall apart around them, and it wouldn't matter. The only thing that did was happening right there in the cab of his rapidly overheating truck. His mouth shifted lower, and the rasp of his stubble against the tender flesh of her neck set off an ache between her legs.

She wanted this man.

In her arms.

In her bed.

In her *life*.

Colby's mind tripped at the thought before she whisked it away. Now was not the time to overthink. She had all night for that. Right now was about Jason and the delicious things he could do with his mouth. She squirmed in his lap, and the resulting moan he issued turned the ache into a raging fire in her blood. He pressed up against her.

"You're going to be the death of me, you know that?" he asked, his raspy voice sending a shiver down her spine. That shiver became an all-out shudder when his lips brushed her ear, whispering what he wanted to do to her...things he *promised* to do to her soon. And Colby planned to hold him to those naughty promises.

Every. Last. One.

A sudden bright light flooded the cab. They sprang apart like two horny teenagers caught making out after curfew and Colby laughed, breathless, as she pressed her fingers against her swollen lips. She had wanted to give him something to think about, and that should've done the trick.

With a triumphant grin, she glanced outside the fogged up passenger's side window and did a double-take when she spotted a familiar car—more specifically, a magenta colored Bug—whip into the wide driveway.

Oh, God.

Colby smoothed her mussed hair as she quickly ran her sleeve along the window, hoping to clear the steam away from her sister's all-knowing gaze. A minute later, Sherry propped an elbow through her opened window and mouthed the word, "Busted."

Gleeful eyebrows—if it were possible for eyebrows to be gleeful—wagged up and down as her sister leaned forward to toss Jason an exaggerated wink. Then with a laugh, she turned off her engine.

Neither of them spoke as Sherry gathered her things and skipped up the drive, stopping to turn and wave before closing the front door. Blood that was already pumping through her body flooded Colby's face. Yep, that had just happened.

She was a grown woman. Hooking up with Jason had been Sherry's idea in the first place, and Colby had no doubt she'd been doing the very same thing on her own date tonight with a waiter from Robicheaux's. But that didn't stop Colby from squeezing her eyes shut and wishing she could rewind time. Biting her lip, Colby stole a glance at Jason from the corner of her eye and found him smirking. "What?"

The smirk became a smile as he combed a hand through his hair. "Just trying to decide if it would've been worse if that had been Cane."

A flare of annoyance piqued at the mention of her brother. Colby still had no clue why he reacted the way he did the other day, or why he thought her love life was any of his business. But she also loved the overbearing brute and knew he had his reasons. They would just have to make sure he never found out about their arrangement.

Going for levity, Colby said, "It's a toss-up. Sherry will taunt me forever, and Cane would've kicked your ass." The smile on his face dimmed and she nudged him with her elbow. "Dude, I was joking. Who cares what Cane thinks? This is about us."

Jason nodded and let out a breath, worry still etched on his forehead as he wrapped his hand around the keys to start the engine. Apparently, the sight of one sibling and the mention of the other was a mood killer. Colby flipped down the visor and checked her makeup in the mirror in the hopes of minimizing the teasing she knew was coming the moment she stepped inside. Then she glanced back at Jason with her hand on the door. "I had fun tonight."

He slid her a boyish grin. "Me, too."

Jason's smiles always did decidedly funny things to her tummy. Squeezing the door handle to keep from launching herself back into his arms, she asked, "Pick this up Monday?"

He took her unoccupied left hand and brought it to his mouth. "I won't be able to think of anything else."

Mission accomplished.

Then he pressed a kiss against her opened palm and Colby's eyelids fluttered.

Now, neither would she.

• • •

Jason deserved a damn medal. Or at the very least, a freaking fist bump. Driving away from Colby tonight, when every fiber of his being screamed for him to go back and pick up where Sherry had interrupted them, had to be one of the hardest things he'd ever done. But he'd done it. Gritting his teeth, fists clenched around the smooth steering wheel, but he'd managed to do it. And despite the cold shower he knew awaited him, he was almost certain it had been the right decision.

But damn it sucked.

As he drove home on autopilot, he told himself that accepting her tempting offer would've destroyed any chance he had with her. All night long, his old man's words replayed in his mind. The puzzle pieces aligned, the game changed, and his plan shifted. Now, a summer fling with Colby was no longer going to be enough. But if Jason had any shot of making her stick around Magnolia Springs at the end of this, he had to play his cards right. He had to get his head on straight and his plan in place. One wrong move, one moment of weakness, and she'd slip through his fingers in a few short months.

At the four-way stop, Jason leaned back against the headrest. She wasn't going to make it easy. Colby Robicheaux was temptation incarnate. And she was a woman on a mission. He reached into the glove compartment, grabbed his pack of spearmint gum, and then pushed his foot down on the accelerator. The rising hum of the engine matched his frustration. He'd been out of the game for a while, but he could still read signals. Especially when they were as loud as Colby's. That woman wanted him all right. Just maybe not in the same ways that he was beginning to want *her*.

Oh, he wanted her physically; that was a damn given. But he also wondered if she could be the right fit for Emma's mother. Watching them together tonight, he knew he couldn't ask for a better person for the role. As for what his dad had implied before, that's where it got sticky. Holding Colby in his arms tonight, looking into those endless smoky gray eyes, a warmth had flickered in his chest. And it scared the living hell out of him.

It was time for him to cool off, regroup, and think up a new strategy. One that, if things went his way, could have a whole new objective in mind. An entire summer sounded long, but with a woman as hurt and stubborn as Colby, time was not his friend.

The flickering sign for Jake's Seafood caught Jason's eye as he made a tight right turn on Stinson. Known for supplying restaurants and boiling aficionados with the biggest and freshest Gulf coast seafood, the weather-battered establishment was like an omen. If he wanted to break through Colby's defenses, the first thing he had to do was get her to fall back in love with Cajun food. The cuisine was part of her heritage. It was a staple of her family's restaurant. And it was a major wall keeping her from healing from the past.

While Jason enjoyed cooking, a true chef he wasn't. A plan like this called for the absolute best. Normally with the new chef in town, Jason would turn to Robicheaux's, but this required an outside job. Copeland's, Acme, Brennan's. Jason needed to call in the big guns.

Next, he would move on to helping her rediscover her love of their city. New Orleans was magical when you let it in. From its people, to its century-old superstitions and traditions, to the art and music that influence every facet of daily life, the city burrows into your soul. Jason would bet his Saints season tickets that though Colby fought it fiercely, New Orleans was still a part of her. Maybe buried deep, but it was in there. Just like the starry-eyed girl he remembered, who wore her heart on her sleeve and believed in love, was still inside her, too.

Jason pulled into his garage and turned off the engine. This plan felt solid. It meant delaying what he wanted, what his body was aching to do, that much longer. But it felt right. Despite what he'd told Colby, he was starting to realize he wasn't in this for a hookup or a casual fling. As much as it sucked, he knew he couldn't take Colby to his bed until she could take a tearless carriage ride with him through the French Quarter—while eating a beignet from Café Du Monde.

With his new plan now firmly, if not begrudgingly, in place, Monday night couldn't come fast enough.

Chapter Eleven

Colby shook out her hands on Jason's doorstep, wishing her crappy day could shake off with the gesture. Lights blazed on the other side of his etched glass door, and from somewhere within she could hear Jason singing along—loudly—to the classic rock blaring over his speakers. He was surprisingly in tune. She grinned, imagining him serenading a simmering pot of something delicious, wiggling his *Kiss the Chef* apron clad hips.

At least one of them was in the proper mood.

While all of the days since their nighttime interlude had dragged like the sluggish bayou behind her family's restaurant, today had sucked the hardest. She just didn't get it. There were *tons* of Italians in the Greater New Orleans area. Her mom's side of the family proved that. So did the yearly Irish/Italian parades and the huge St. Joseph's Day altars residents built city-wide. But make a few small changes to the menu, switching out one or two hardcore Cajun classics with fresh, updated Italian ones, and the natives go crazy. Apparently, an act like that was akin to sacrilege.

Colby had hoped changing up the menu would bring

fresh lifeblood into the restaurant. She'd also hoped it would make it easier to stomach the kitchen during the next few months. Day in and day out cooking the same recipes she'd learned alongside her father was starting to take its toll. But she hadn't come home to ruin her family's legacy, so she'd just have to suck it up. If the people wanted Cajun food, then by God, Cajun food they would get. Even if it killed her.

She rolled back her shoulders. If she weren't such a workaholic, she wouldn't have known there was an issue. Most women would've spent their day off primping when they had a hot date. Instead, her perfectionist-self just *had* to go in to check over the day's prep work, leading to her overhearing Cane and Sherry's hushed conversation. Listening to them worry about her, question her decisions, yet agree to believe in her regardless of customer complaints had sealed the deal. She loved her siblings more than air and this wasn't about being selfish. She could think with her head and not her heart, and doing that, everything would go back to normal tomorrow.

Tonight, however, she was dressed to impress and standing outside her childhood crush's home. Wasting way too much energy thinking about work and depressing guilt. Worrying about the restaurant could wait until morning—*now* it was time to focus on more enticing, enjoyable thoughts. Such as rocking Jason's world.

She rang the doorbell.

The radio cut off mid-song and she watched through the glass as Jason walked up. The eager smile on his face was the absolute sexiest thing she had ever seen.

"You're late," he teased after opening the door. He leaned in to brush his lips across her cheek, and her knees nearly buckled at the clean scent of soap and aftershave. He slid his hands around hers and tugged her inside. "I was starting to think you were gonna stand me up."

Colby laughed, the annoyance of the day already lifting off her shoulders. "Everyone knows a woman has to make an entrance." She inhaled deeply, trying to get a hint of what he'd cooked. Not picking anything up, she asked, "What's for dinner?"

A muscle clenching and unclenching in his jaw was her only clue—and not much of one—before he said, "That's a surprise."

Curious, she let him pull her farther inside. But instead of heading toward the dining room as she'd expected, or even toward the more intimate kitchen table, he led her into the living room. He gently backed her against the leather sofa. "Take a seat."

Okay. No need for concern here, she told herself, sinking into the soft cushions. Just because she absolutely hated surprises, didn't trust them, and hadn't had a good one since her life fell apart twelve years ago, she didn't need to go mental. This was a date, and dates were supposed to be fun. Spontaneous. She could go with the flow.

Besides, it was possible he wanted to talk before they ate. Or watch a movie, breaking out the TV trays like they did when they were kids. She could handle that. It wasn't romantic, but she didn't need romance. She and Jason were just two old friends hanging out, throwing in some much needed benefits, and getting their freak on.

Do people still even say that?

Colby shook her head, her inner-monologue only confirming how long it had been for her. And how badly she needed this. She put on her sexiest smile and glanced up at him, feeling it freeze on her face when she glimpsed the object in his hands.

A black silk blindfold.

Now *that* was the type of surprise she could get behind.

"And the night takes a turn for the intriguing." She bit her lower lip as Jason started rubbing the soft material between his long, work-roughened fingers. She cleared her throat and asked, "But shouldn't we eat first? You know, shore up our strength?"

Jason chuckled. "This *is* for eating." At her nose crinkle of confusion, he sank to his knees in front of her and said, "I'm going to feed you blindfolded."

Oh my.

She didn't know what she had expected from tonight, but this certainly wasn't it. Not that she was complaining. She knew very well how sensual food could be. And how turning off one sense heightened all the others. Colby swallowed hard as Jason leaned forward, gently stretching the elastic band of the blindfold.

"Do you mind?" His voice was a husky whisper at her ear. All she could manage was a small shake of her head. Already her pulse was taking flight and heat was pooling in her belly.

What will it be like later? Was it possible to self-combust from anticipation alone?

He chuckled lightly under his breath, most likely hearing the pant of her breath. She'd be embarrassed if she weren't so damn excited. As he secured the band around her head, the spicy scent of his aftershave flooded her senses, making everything electric. Goose bumps skittered down her spine as his palm smoothed the back of her hair. Just before tugging the silky material over her eyes, Jason looked into them and said, "*Bon appétit*, Chef."

A pop of a joint and the rustle of fabric told Colby that he was moving. The pad of his footsteps on the carpet grew faint, letting her know he was walking away, probably into the kitchen to get their dinner. She still couldn't pick up any scents, but then, the thrum of expectation coursing through her body made it hard to concentrate. Soon those same soft footsteps returned, growing louder as Jason neared. "I hope you don't mind, but I outsourced dinner tonight."

She heard the *plop* of something heavy hit the ground. "Was that a brick?"

He chuckled again and the sound made her shiver. "Just my basket of provisions. This is a three-course tasting."

She stopped herself from saying that all she wanted to taste at that moment was *him*. The admission seemed a bit over the top—even if it was the truth. Instead, she said, "Can't wait to see what you brought me."

The sounds of preparations stilled and then the warmth of Jason's hands pressed on her thighs. "Colby, before we start, I just want you to know that I care about you. And all I ask is that you trust me."

"I do trust you." Right now, in this moment, she couldn't think of anyone she trusted more.

He squeezed the sides of her legs and moved away, taking the heat of his skin along with him. A clink of glass meeting glass then, "Open your mouth and suck."

Colby barked a laugh. The teasing tone of his voice told her he knew exactly how that had sounded. "So that's how you're gonna play it, huh?"

His seductive whisper came at her ear. "Gotta keep you on your toes."

Heat zipped through her core as he grazed her jawline with a kiss, then he leaned away with a laugh, deep and throaty. The teasing helped. Suddenly, muscles in her lower back that she hadn't realized were tense began to relax. Colby wrapped her lips around the straw she knew was waiting, and proceeded to suck. The familiar smell of rum, then the sweet bite of fruit—cherry or passion fruit—hit her palate.

It was smooth, refreshing. Tart. And then she knew exactly what it was. A hurricane. To be specific, a Pat O'Brien's Hurricane, if she had to guess. It was delicious, one of her favorites when she was in high school and flaunting her fake ID. And just like that, the memories began.

High school graduation. Her dad beaming with pride. After shutting down the restaurant for a private party, he'd hired a limo to drive her friends and family to Bourbon Street. Normally, hanging with your parents wasn't exactly "cool," but her friends had always loved them. Especially her dad. He could hold his own, throwing back more drinks than they could, and he had deep pockets. Colby loved having him there because she adored him. The first stop they'd made that night was the back patio of Pat O's where in front of the landmark Flaming Fountain the group guzzled hurricane after hurricane, laughing and dancing.

Colby clamped her already closed eyes tighter.

A cold sweat prickled the nape of her neck as she tore her lips from the straw. "Jason?" That one taste of hurricane revealed exactly what kind of meal he'd prepared.

"Shh," he said, running his hands along her arms. "Just trust me. Please?"

It was the hesitant please that got her. She tried to relax the fists in her lap. Heaviness had replaced the desire once pooling in her stomach, but she didn't *want* to be angry. If she was angry, they'd never get to dessert—the kind that she'd actually come there for.

She trusted Jason. His actions were severely misguided, and about the furthest thing from a turn on the man could get, but he meant well. She knew that.

And there was safety in this experience. He was here with her. The memories were going to burst through—there was no stopping them now—but he would be here to catch her.

Protect her. Hold her. And hopefully in the end, kiss them all away.

Colby slowly nodded. "Let me have another sip." If she was going to do this, at least the buzz would help dull the pain.

This time, when the slight sting of rum hit the back of her throat, she was prepared—this drink had an extra shot. Good, that would help. The sip went down easily so she took another. That was the danger in hurricanes, and the reason teenage boys loved supplying their dates with drink after drink. They tasted so good the effects snuck up on you.

After draining what had to be half the glass, she raised her head. Things were definitely fuzzier. "What's for round two?"

Warm, calloused hands suddenly cradled her face as Jason's firm lips pressed against hers. She latched onto his arms. Her mouth parted, reeling from the abrupt change in direction the evening had taken, and he nipped her upper lip between his teeth. Her breath caught and a chill shot down her arms as his tongue rimmed the inside of her mouth, licking the remnants of the fruity drink from her lips. She snatched the fabric of his cotton T-shirt, twisting it in her hands.

If this was what awaited her after every round, she could handle just about anything.

"God, you're sexy," he rasped, pulling his talented mouth away. His hands slipped from her face and slid down her arms. "And strong. You can do this, you know. I've got you."

Colby nodded. Whether she could do this or not remained to be determined, but she wanted to see it through. Especially if she had to cook these meals for the rest of the summer, she needed to try. And the fact that Jason cared enough to want this for her made something in her chest ache, in a good way.

She let out a heavy breath as the sounds of him preparing her next course broke the silence. Stretching her hearing, she tried to get a handle on what it was he was doing, trying to guess what lay ahead. But she got nothing.

A moment later, "Open up."

Hesitant but resolute, she did as Jason asked. And the first thing to touch her tongue was crisp, crunchy French bread. She moaned. That was something New Orleans always got right. The sharp crust of the outside, and the airy softness of the inside. It kicked hoagie bread's ass. Then she detected the nuttiness of cheese and as she closed her mouth around the entire bite, the sweet luxurious lump of crab.

She chewed, waiting for the sting of hurt and pain to come. But it didn't. The flavors were familiar and a series of memories played in rapid succession, but the ache was dulled. *Thank God.* Her spine relaxed against the cushions. The day of the competition had been a shock, tasting the spices and recipes of her past after so long. And at the restaurant, in her father's kitchen, sampling the food to ensure the quality was a responsibility always done begrudgingly, in the shadow of the man who had broken her heart.

But tonight was different. This was with Jason. He was safe, and he understood.

So the memories continued with each new taste. The crunch of fried crawfish tails, the velvet tenderness of the linguine. The tang of the garlic and the smoke of the Andouille. All brought memories of meals she'd eaten, dates she had gone on, meals she had prepared. And they brought memories of her dad. Not the bad ones this time—only the good.

As Colby closed her mouth around a forkful of étouffée, the punch of herbs and cayenne enveloped her. She was no longer in Jason's living room, but right back in her childhood kitchen, closing her eyes as she tasted her dad's recipe. She heard the laughter in her daddy's thick Cajun-accented voice as he asked, "Good stuff, *cher*?" Her younger self giggled with a nod.

And then the pain came.

It lanced through her heart, tearing through the hurt of the past twelve years, and adding intense longing for her dad. Undoubtedly, the man had made some *huge* mistakes. But in all the calls she'd never taken, in the years of messages he'd left on her machine, he'd said he had ended the affair. For twelve years, he apologized to Colby's voice mail. Telling her he loved her, wishing she'd come home. Saying how proud he was of everything she had accomplished, and confessing how much he missed her.

Colby had never taken his calls. She had never forgiven him in person. And now she never could.

Jason pulled her up and over onto his lap, wrapping her in his strong arms. She hadn't even realized she was sobbing. "I'm here," he said, ripping off her blindfold and pressing his forehead against hers. "It's all right."

But it wasn't. And it might not ever be. Her dad was dead. Reconciliation was impossible. And it was all her fault.

Colby curled into a ball on his lap, bringing her legs to her chest and burrowing herself under his chin. Dessert would have to wait for another night. She closed her eyes and Jason tightened his grip around her, letting her cry.

Eventually her breathing stabilized and exhaustion swept her under, yet he continued to hold her. And, as Colby absorbed the comfort of Jason's warmth and his strength, she realized that she was in serious trouble. Because if she wasn't very careful, if she didn't guard her heart, she would find herself falling hard for this amazing man. Again.

• • •

"Dad, you're hanging with Colby and me?"

Jason rubbed the back of his neck. He glanced at the front door to Robicheaux's, wishing he could see through the wood. Would it be weird if he told Emma yes? It hadn't even been a full twenty-four hours since seeing Colby, but already he was aching to hold her again.

Last night's dinner had been emotional. The second Colby showed up at his door, Jason knew that she'd had a different agenda for the night. One that was as opposite from his as humanly possible. He'd nearly scrapped his good intentions when she made that comment about the blindfold, but he stuck to his guns. And as hard as it was watching Colby cry, he was glad he did, because at the end of those tears, Jason saw a glimpse of healing. She'd confided about her father and her regrets, and even thanked him for the food intervention — albeit with a saucy grin.

His plan was working.

Barging in on his daughter's one-on-one time to check on Colby may be a little pathetic, but he was surprisingly okay with that. As long as he got to see her. Touch her. And maybe, when their audience wasn't looking, steal a kiss or two from the sexy chef.

"I thought I'd see what junior sous-chefs do in a real kitchen," he said, ruffling his daughter's hair. "You don't mind my staying for a while, do you?"

Emma's face lit with a sly smile—though the reason behind it was anything but. Knowing how much she loved Colby already *almost* had Jason backpedaling to his truck. If he weren't so confident about how this would play out, it would have. He'd be crushed if Emma grew attached only to have Vegas yank Colby back at the end of the summer, but this was going to work. It had to. If not for him and *whatever* closeness he was starting to feel for her, Jason needed Colby to stay for his daughter.

Emma latched onto his arm. "Nope. I know Colby would *love* to see you."

He choked back a laugh. Subtlety was not her strong suit. Choosing not to comment on her presumption, he waved his free hand toward the entrance. "Then lead on, Chef Landry."

Jason fell in step behind Emma's bouncing ponytail, going over his strategy. Dinner had gone better than he'd dared expect. But his mission was far from complete. He needed to begin the second phase of his strategy. Secure another date. And that was the game plan for this afternoon.

Emma tugged open the door, the *ding* of bells giving away their entrance. A young family with a sleeping baby looked up from their meal along the wall of windows. Beside them, an elderly man flipped the page of his newspaper. Out on the deck, a group looked as though they were just finishing a lunch meeting. Soft jazz played overhead. Robicheaux's was square in the middle of its afternoon lull, the slow time between the lunch rush and crazy dinner crowd. Perfect for what he had in mind.

As he and his daughter made their way toward the back, his best friend's disembodied head peered around the kitchen door. "Hey, Em. You ready for that job yet?"

"Not yet, Uncle Cane," she answered with a roll of her eyes. "I'm still only twelve."

"Oh, that's right. I keep forgetting. You're just getting so *old*." Cane winked at his goddaughter and then switched his attention to Jason. "You here for free labor, too?"

"Thought I'd see what you people were filling my daughter's head with. Maybe steal a free meal while I was at it."

Cane stepped through the pocket door, scratching his stubbled jaw. "The food is my sister's domain, but something tells me she'll hook you up." His mouth tightened; clearly, he was still conflicted on his best friend and little sister *hooking up*. But then he shook his head and said, "She's been going to town in the kitchen all morning."

Jason's ears perked up. He couldn't help hoping their culinary adventure was the inspiration for her newfound zeal in the kitchen. A huge-ass smile broke across his face, and Cane's eyes sharpened.

"Interesting."

Emma turned to look at Jason too, and he quickly wiped the smirk off his face.

"What? That's good, right?" he asked. "I'm just happy to hear it's going well."

Jason smiled, adding a pointed look that clearly told his friend to drop it. So far, with help from his parents, he'd kept Emma from learning about his date with Colby—and he wanted to keep it that way. Right now, all Emma knew was that Colby had gone on the camping trip, at her request, and then attended her assembly, again at her invitation. Her hopes of a relationship working out between them were already high enough *without* her knowing anything was actually going on. The last thing Jason needed was for his friend to nose around now and stir up his daughter's curiosity.

With a discreet nod, Cane poked his head through the kitchen door. "Anyone order a preteen chef and a fire captain?" He glanced back at Emma and grinned. "If not, I'm tossing them into the bayou."

From inside the kitchen Jason heard a squeal, then an exasperated *shh*, followed by Sherry's unmistakable laugh. A moment later, both women scooted out behind their brother.

"Hey, Emma," Colby said nonchalantly. "Here to learn more about the restaurant biz?"

She nodded. "Sorry for not calling first. Dad said you wouldn't mind."

"Don't be silly, you're welcome here any time."

Silence fell. One that Sherry miraculously didn't feel the need to fill with endless chatter. Colby wiped her hand on a stained white towel, looking at Emma and the straggling customers—anywhere but at *him*.

Jason had seen the woman upset. He'd seen her laughing. He'd seen her stumbling and confident and angry. But he couldn't remember the last time he'd seen her nervous. Instinct told him that her being nervous around *him* might just be a very good thing. And the exultant look on Sherry's face confirmed it.

Colby shifted her feet. Her eyes finally met his and twin flushes of pink blossomed on her cheeks. It was adorable— and a hell of a turn on. Fiddling with the buttons on her chef jacket, she asked, "Dropping her off?"

"Actually, I thought I'd hang around." He leaned back on his heels and grinned. "If you don't mind, that is."

Her blush deepened. "Of course I—*we* don't mind." She jutted her thumb in the direction of the kitchen and widened her eyes. "Emma, wanna introduce your dad to the world of prep work?"

"Awesome."

Colby wagged her head for Emma to follow, and all four of them walked through the pocket door. She looked around at her audience with a frown. "Sherry, don't you have some tables to check?"

"Nope," she answered with a sweet smile. "All cleared out and taken care of. They're camping."

She pressed her lips together and turned to her brother. "And you? Don't you have numbers to crunch? A bar to stock?"

"Already crunched," Cane said, pushing himself up on a countertop, settling in. "Already stocked." He raised an eyebrow, dark eyes shining with amusement. Jason scratched the side of his jaw, trying to hide his smile.

This was why he loved being an honorary Robicheaux. He wouldn't trade his own family for anything in the world; he just counted it as a blessing to be a part of both. The Robicheaux family teased as fiercely as they loved. They stuck their noses in each other's business, and they didn't even try to hide it. Colby was obviously flustered and didn't want an audience, and that was exactly why they stayed. Even with his lingering concerns, Cane couldn't pass up an opportunity to make his sister squirm. His best friend looked at Jason over Colby's head and grinned.

"All right, then." Blowing her bangs off her forehead, Colby pulled a binder down from a shelf on the wall. "These are the lists for the tasks that must be completed daily, or before each shift. Depending on the night or the shift, we have three or four cooks back here, including me, who are responsible for getting these things done. As you see, most of these are already completed. So, Emma, what should we do next?"

"Um…check the food prep sheet?"

"Excellent," she affirmed. Pure delight lit up his daughter's face and Jason's chest tightened. "You're a fast learner, girl. You're gonna be running this place soon."

"I've been trying to rope her into a job here for years," Cane replied, lightly swatting Emma with a clean dishcloth. "She *says* she has to finish school first."

They all laughed and as the gentle teasing and outright pranks continued, the worry lines on Colby's face softened. The five of them, along with the other staff, readied the kitchen for the dinner service and then they moved into the front of the house for wait-staff prep.

It was during the time Emma was instructing her old man

on the proper way to roll silverware that she spoke up. "Y'all should totally cater the firehouse celebration next month."

"The firehouse celebration?" Colby asked. "What's that?"

"It's gonna be *huge*," she answered, balancing the last wrapped silverware on her self-created pyramid. "Dad even got the Joey Thomas Band to play!"

"Thus making me a hero," Jason declared with a grin. "Actually, that's a great idea, Em. Robicheaux's should cater—if you're interested."

Colby's teeth sunk into her full bottom lip. Her eyes widened as she turned to Sherry. "We could introduce the new items."

He grimaced. Colby's new *Italian* items had been the talk of the town for weeks—and not in a good way. Seeing the look of concern on his face, the youngest Robicheaux explained. "Tapas, but with a Cajun twist. Chica came in this morning bursting with new ideas."

Cajun tapas, he thought, catching Colby's eye. Jason liked it. Even more, he liked that their dinner together had evidently inspired it.

Phase one was officially complete.

"What's the party for?" she asked.

"A century of service," Jason said with pride. "Magnolia Springs Fire Department was first established as a volunteer department a hundred years ago. We're celebrating our years of service to the community with games, jumpers for the kids, fire truck tours—"

"And bands," Emma interrupted.

"And live music," he added. "We were just gonna do ice cream and drinks, but a full spread would be great."

Cane folded his arms across the back of the booth. "Will all the firefighters be there?"

Jason couldn't help but smile at his friend's interest. "You mean Angelle? Yeah, she'll be there."

The question was where *wasn't* Angelle these days. Since her surprise—and frankly, uncomfortable—pop-in during his and Cane's dinner the other night, the woman was everywhere. At the firehouse, at the gym. He half expected her to show up at Emma's school. She didn't give off any stalker vibes, and she really was a sweet girl, but he wasn't interested...and she clearly was.

Colby narrowed her eyes as she looked back and forth between them. "Who's Angelle?"

"Just a woman I work with," he quickly replied. There was no way in hell he was letting worry over Angelle screw things up between them. "No one important."

A strange look settled on her face and Jason rushed to change the topic. "So, I'm curious. If weekends are so busy in the restaurant business, when do chefs ever get time off?"

Obviously, he knew she had Mondays off. But he wasn't waiting a whole week to take her out. Cane and Sherry exchanged a look.

"It varies restaurant to restaurant, I suppose," Colby answered. "For myself, I normally take off Mondays and Thursdays. Some weeks I change it up and take off Wednesday instead, but those days are typically the slowest."

Quickly going over the calendar in his head, Jason nodded. He could work with Thursday.

"Hey, Bug, do you mind running to the truck? I borrowed *Talladega Nights* from Uncle Cane and forgot it in there."

His daughter was no idiot. The same sly smile she wore when they'd arrived snuck back on her face, and she nodded. "Sure thing." She dashed across the restaurant without another word.

Sherry sank into the booth across from him, plopping her chin in her hand with an exultant look. "Don't let me interrupt."

Jason's lips twitched in amusement. There was no point hiding anything. Sherry already caught them making out, and Cane knew the score. Or, what he *thought* was the score. With a quick glance at his friend, Jason swiped the sugar container from Colby's fingertips and said, "Thursday night I'm taking you out. A real date this time, out of the house. By some miracle, the both of us are off on the same night and we're jumping on it."

A mischievous spark lit her gray eyes. "Oh we are, huh?" A smirk twitched her lips, telling exactly what kind of *jumping* Colby had in mind. And when he nodded, at both the question and her unspoken innuendo, the smirk turned wicked.

Jason fisted his hands by his side, barely keeping himself from capturing those twitching lips with his own. But he could afford to be patient. If phase two went anywhere near as well as phase one, by the end of the night Thursday that wicked smirk would be the *only* thing Colby had on.

Chapter Twelve

What kind of underwear did one wear when dressing for a night of seduction? So far, Colby had worn the lacy black ensemble during the first botched attempt after Emma's assembly and her purple satin during the second debacle at Jason's house. Obviously, the sexier the outfit the better. But when the end goal was to shed the clothes as quickly as possible, wouldn't it make more sense simply to go without?

Colby choked on her swig of Diet Mountain Dew. Even in her own thoughts, she couldn't let herself go there. With her luck, her dress would bunch up at dinner and she'd moon the entire restaurant. No, as daring as the notion was, it was best to stick with traditional come-hither attire. And luckily, she'd ransacked Victoria's Secret last week for this very reason. Surveying the array of options in her lingerie drawer, she selected a red lace push-up bra and matching panties. If that didn't say *hey baby,* she didn't know what did.

After donning the sexy garments and sliding a flirty black dress over her head, she brushed out her hair and reapplied her lipstick. A spritz of perfume later, she was ready to roll. With a few minutes remaining before Jason was expected,

Colby slid onto a bar stool in the kitchen and grabbed her legal pad, jotting down notes for her latest recipe: crawfish beignets.

Ever since their emotional dinner, she had been riding a high at the restaurant. The smells and tastes of the kitchen were now welcomed, instead of endured. Twists on old recipes kept springing to mind. One night hadn't erased all the pain of her past. She wasn't ready to say she'd completely forgiven her father. But she *was* able to embrace the food of her childhood and her culture. And that was a big first step.

A loud rap on the door startled her and sent her pulse skittering. Shoving the pad back in the drawer, Colby pushed to her feet and fanned her face, wondering, not for the first time, why she couldn't be the smooth, confident one for once. She closed her eyes, counted to five, fanned some more, and let out a deep breath. *Game time.*

Sauntering through the hall, she added a sway to her hips. True, no one was there to witness the performance, but it did put what she hoped was a sexy smile on her face. She raised her chin and tugged open the door. "Why hello there, Handsome — "

And that's as far as Colby got. Her eyes widened, drinking Jason in. Oh, he was handsome all right. Sinfully so. And if she hadn't skipped lunch that day due to a nervous tummy, she'd be hauling him inside and saying to hell with dinner. He was dressed in dark slacks and a white button down shirt. The tail untucked, the sleeves rolled up, and the top button left undone. At the expanse of toned, tanned skin, her mouth went dry. *Holy Forearms, this man is hot!* She blinked and raised her eyes to meet his amused gaze.

"You, Miss Robicheaux, are stunning." Under Jason's sweeping appraisal, Colby's flesh tingled as if he'd stroked it. His eyes came to rest on the deep V-neck of her dress, and a slow smile stretched across his face. "Are you ready?"

Are you?

Nodding, she grabbed her bag from the entry table, still rendered mute. Last night Jason had texted her, giving no clues as to what lay ahead other than she needed to pack an overnight bag. When Sherry had shamelessly read this over her shoulder, she had cackled with delight.

"Here, let me," he said, slipping the bag from her fingers. He slid his other hand behind her back, leading her out the door. She loved that he was a physical touch kind of guy. Not afraid to hold her hand, to brand her with his palm. It was comforting and thrilling and completely addictive. His hand stayed on the small of her back while she locked up and as they walked toward his truck. He opened her door, like the true Southern gentleman he was, and then sealed her inside.

Watching him stroll around the front of the truck, Colby reminded herself for what felt like the millionth time that this wasn't truly a date. That it was two friends hanging out, grabbing dinner, and taking advantage of the unmistakable attraction snapping between them. But the more she tried to convince herself that her heart was safe, the more she realized it was a lie. And she hated liars.

If she were to be honest with herself—truly and completely honest—she'd admit that she was falling in love with Jason. If she'd ever truly fallen *out* of it. And the more time they spent together—the longer she was exposed to his smiles, to his laughter, to his kindness—the more tempted she was to believe in happily ever afters again. This summer was changing her. And she wasn't sure if it was for the better.

"So, where you taking me, Captain?" she asked when Jason hopped behind the wheel.

He shot her a look as he cranked the engine. "Do you really think I'd ruin forty-eight hours of mystery now? I've worked hard, woman. All will be revealed in time."

She scrunched her nose. "Not even a tiny hint?"

"Anyone ever tell you that surprises can be romantic?" he asked, backing out of the driveway. "I've heard some women find them to be a turn on."

Colby snorted. "If I get any more turned on, this truck might just combust."

It took a moment for her to realize she'd actually spoken that thought aloud. When she did, she smacked her hand over her mouth.

Jason chuckled. "Well then," he said with a wicked grin. "Challenge accepted."

Somehow, Colby managed not to embarrass herself, or set fire to the truck, during the rest of the drive. But that was more likely due to her preoccupation than her linguistic skills. As soon as Jason had turned on to the Causeway, she'd known where he was taking her. And with each mile driven to downtown New Orleans, her mind had tripped over memories of field trips, former dates, high school dances, and family gatherings. Over the years, she'd made the occasional trip back home. There were a handful of Christmases, one botched Thanksgiving, her mother's funeral three years ago, and then her dad's only two months ago. But in all those visits, she'd never ventured outside their small hometown. Colby hadn't actually set foot in the city of New Orleans since she was eighteen years old.

As they drove down I-10, she kept her eyes open for changes. The lingering effects of Katrina could still be felt, some more noticeable than others. But the regrowth, the improvements, were everywhere, and that made her heart swell with pride. Southerners were made of strong stuff for sure, but New Orleanians embodied determination. They never gave up on their beloved Saints—and that unfailing belief got them the Super Bowl. And the stubborn faith bled into their homes and communities. Most of the people who evacuated came right back and rebuilt on the same plot of ground the levee waters destroyed.

Colby had watched the footage along with the rest of the world and received updates from her family. But seeing the rejuvenation in person, breathing the same air again...it felt right.

It felt like *home.*

And that, she suspected, was the whole point of tonight's venture. Jason was definitely up to something. First with the food the other night, and now with the city walk down memory lane. It wasn't unheard of for locals to make the twenty-minute trek downtown, but her intuition was screaming that the man had a plan. And the thrum of energy in her veins said that it was working.

Damn him.

Colby grinned despite herself. Jason noticed. "I take it you approve?" he asked, glancing over as he turned onto Royal Street.

She nodded, prepared to tell him just how much she approved, when her breath caught. They had turned again, this time onto Orleans Street, and the truck slowed to a stop in front of the Bourbon Orleans.

Flags waved overhead. Wrought iron balconies and charming painted shutters whispered Southern elegance. This almost two hundred year old building was the site of Colby's high school prom. It was where she'd envisioned getting married someday. She snuck a glance at Jason. Could he have known that?

The man in question winked at her as he handed the keys over to the valet. "Your room awaits, m'lady."

"You knew, didn't you?"

"It's possible your sister gave me some suggestions," he admitted with a grin. He reached over and gently grasped her chin between his thumb and forefinger, the lighthearted expression he'd worn during the drive fading into a look of complete sincerity. "Colby, I'm not above asking for help if it means making this night perfect for you."

For a moment, she forgot to breathe. It was possible her heart forgot to beat. She simply stared into Jason's melted caramel eyes. There was a message swirling in their depths, and although she wasn't entirely sure what it was, butterflies began twirling in her stomach anyway.

A softened cough popped the bubble that had formed around them. The young valet stood at the driver's side door, key in hand, patiently waiting for them to step out. Heat flooded her cheeks when the man's lips twitched, and she quickly opened her door and hopped onto the sidewalk.

As Jason handed their baggage over to the bell staff, Colby breathed in the city. To the left stood the historic St. Louis Cathedral, and to the right, couples were strolling down the world famous Bourbon Street. At the corner, a two-piece band played a jazz tune, the old man's raspy voice encouraging curious children to dance. Everything you could possibly want to see or experience in the city was within walking distance. Growing up, she hadn't gotten many chances to play tourist, but she had a feeling tonight that was exactly what Jason had in mind. And she couldn't wait.

Inside, the hotel was exactly as she remembered. Gorgeous crystal chandeliers, thick opulent columns, and an extended white tile walkway outlined in smooth black marble. The lobby screamed decadence. Alcoves to the left and right featured lavish furniture and lush, patterned rugs that begged guests to rest their feet and soak it in. As tempting as the thought was, Colby was a woman on a mission.

Jason held out his hand, and she took it.

Waiting as he checked them in and arranged for the luggage delivery to their room, Colby couldn't help feeling as though she was Julia Roberts in *Pretty Woman*. No, she wasn't a high-class hooker. And sure, she had stayed in hotels just as fancy, if not fancier, than this in Vegas. But standing in the lobby of the Bourbon Orleans, she felt overwhelmed. In over her head. And as if at the end of the night, her life could change.

Like the main character Vivian, Colby hadn't expected or needed much from her time with Jason. She'd imagined hot trysts and stolen moments. Instead, he was giving her luxury and romance.

The warmth of Jason's hand snapped her back to reality. He nodded toward the exit. "Judging by the growling noises coming from your stomach on the ride over, I'd say the lady is starved." He flashed a grin when she winced. "Ready for surprise number two?"

"It's impolite to remark on bodily functions," she replied with mock annoyance. Then she jabbed him in the ribs with her elbow. "And yes, *please*. Feed me."

He took her hand and slid it into the crook of his arm. "Right this way."

The *click* of her heels on the lobby tile and then the paved sidewalk of Orleans kept time with her pulse. She didn't know where he was taking her, but she knew if the hotel was any indication, she was in for a treat. At the corner, they took a right onto Bourbon. People stood on the beautiful wrought iron balconies holding beads and toasting the crowds below. She and Jason shared a smile at the tipsy couple walking in front of them. It was forever five o'clock in the French Quarter.

It was after the quick right onto St. Ann Street and then the right onto Royal that Colby laughed. "Are you walking me in circles, Mr. Landry?"

"A bit of misdirection perhaps," he said with a chuckle. "Have to make sure you get the full experience. We have a few minutes to kill before our reservation, and another surprise is up after dinner. I wanted you to at least glimpse Bourbon in case we're"—he bit his lip and shot her a heated look—"eager to return to our room for *dessert* later."

Oh yeah. Bring on dessert.

She nodded as delicious anticipation tightened her stomach. "Excellent call."

Through lust-dazed eyes, Colby turned back to the city before her. Paintings of all shapes, sizes, and styles by local artists lined the fence outside St. Louis Cathedral. They slowed as they admired the art.

"This would look awesome in Robicheaux's."

Jason glanced over at the giant crawfish playing a jazz bass guitar in a swirl of bright blues and purple music notes. He grinned. "He kinda looks like Cane."

She looked again and laughed. "I haven't seen him play in a while, but you're absolutely right. I have to get it."

"Here, let me," he said, reaching into his back pocket for his wallet. She opened her mouth to argue and he pressed a quick kiss against her lips. "I insist."

The artist handed him his change and then smiled as she asked, "Local or tourist?" while she wrapped the canvas in plastic.

Jason tuned to Colby who answered, "Local."

The man beside her tensed, and when he took the packaged artwork from the artist's outstretched hands, a satisfied smile stretched across his face.

At the corner of Saint Peter, he tossed money in a musician's opened guitar case. Setting the painting beside it, he took Colby's hand and twirled her in a slow circle. Tugging her close he whispered, "Dance with me."

The world shrank to the two of them, and the sultry sound of a blues guitar. Jason's hips brushed hers. Their eyes locked. And Colby was lost. A goner. As he slid his hand around her waist, guiding her left hand behind his neck with the other, she wondered how she ever thought she could do this without falling head over heels for him again. The boy of her childhood had been fantasy worthy. The man he'd become was real—battle tested and flawed, but still devastatingly perfect for her.

Neither of them spoke as they swayed to the rasp of the singer's voice, the intoxicating thrum of his harmonica. They didn't need to. She was pretty sure her feelings were written all over her face. She was exposed, vulnerable. And torn between wanting to believe the promise she thought she saw in Jason's eyes and needing to steel her heart against it.

He made her want to believe that they could be different. That he could stay faithful and they could have a real shot. Loosening the binds around her heart would be taking a giant leap; she'd be abandoning her entire belief system. But Jason Landry may just be worth it.

The song ended. Drawing oxygen into her parched lungs, Colby turned to thank the musician. The old gentleman tipped his hat and gave her a sweet, missing tooth smile. "Y'all have a nice night now."

Chapter Thirteen

The Court of Two Sisters had been just as magical as Colby remembered. Her parents had taken here there for her thirteenth birthday, and then again for their famous jazz brunch when she turned sixteen. The restaurant's secluded brick patio, the tranquil mosaic fountain, and the canopy of trees lit with twinkle lights always made her feel like she was stepping inside the pages of a fairy tale. As she and Jason dined on fried oysters Rockefeller and juicy barbecue shrimp, a three-piece jazz band serenaded them. If she hadn't already decided she was in love with the man, the romantic setting might just have pushed her over the edge.

After dinner they strolled down Toulouse Street and then onto Decatur, past the familiar sights of Jackson Square. Clutching the painting he'd bought for her, Jason led Colby past the front of the Cathedral. When she realized they were heading in the direction of Café Du Monde, she bumped him with her hip. "I thought you said dessert was at the hotel," she said with an exaggerated frown.

It was entirely possible she was more than a little inebriated.

Jason laughed and brushed his lips across her temple.

"Oh, baby, that's still on. This is just a snack. I have big plans for dessert."

A fresh onslaught of desire incited by the look in his eyes mixed with the rum already floating in her veins, and it was all Colby could do not to tackle him on the street. Instead, she followed as he got an order of beignets to go and then walked up to a mule-drawn carriage.

"Private tour for Landry," Jason said, sliding his driver's license out of his wallet. He handed it along with a folded piece of paper to the flamboyantly dressed driver.

"Hey boy," Colby whispered to the sleepy looking mule. The mule responded by pooping into the bag attached to its backside. *Lovely.* Jason laughed and she sent him a wry smile. "It appears I have an interesting effect on the male species."

"That you do." He kissed her lips and then handed her up into the carriage. "Now," he said, settling beside her, "it's *very* important that we enjoy this ride together while eating these." He opened the bag of beignets and pulled out a big, fluffy, powdered-sugar-coated treat.

"Very important?" she asked, eyeing the pastry with amusement.

Jason nodded and leaned close to her ear. "Trust me. After we do this, I'm prepared to ravage you in our room."

Without another word, Colby snatched the beignet from his hands and took a huge bite. Sweet, airy dough hit her taste buds and her eyes rolled back in her head. "*Mmm,*" she moaned, taking another bite. "Oh my God, that is good."

She opened her eyes when she heard Jason groan. His hungry gaze was riveted on her mouth. And when her tongue darted out for the sugar that clung to her lips, he drew a sharp breath through his nose. In a strained voice, he told the driver, "We're ready."

Obviously, the man had a plan. And she was trying to be

grateful for all the thought he had put into their night. But as romantic as the carriage ride was, and as good as it felt to ride down the streets playing tourist in the city she'd missed (even if she never admitted it to herself), what Colby really wanted was to thank the driver for his efforts, jump out of the carriage, and race back to the hotel for Jason's dessert.

What she settled for, however, was the seductive graze of his fingers along the inside of her thigh. The slow skim of his nose along her throat. And the sound of his harsh breathing in her ear, telling her he wanted this as badly as she did.

Finally, the ride came to a stop back where they began. Jason practically threw a tip at the driver before grasping her hand and hailing a nearby cab. "Bourbon Orleans," he growled, ushering her inside.

"Bourbon Orleans? You know that's only—"

"I know," Jason interrupted, causing Colby to giggle. "This is faster."

The cab driver craned his neck around with a puzzled look. But after taking in the pair of them, he grinned. "Gotcha."

Five minutes later, they were back in their hotel room, tearing at each other's clothes.

Colby's hip bumped into a tray of chocolate covered strawberries. Room service must've brought them, but she'd had enough food for one evening. Lips followed fingers down the buttons of Jason's shirt, eager to see and taste the muscles she'd so far only gotten to imagine. She pushed the sides open and threw the garment on the floor.

She pressed her mouth over his racing heart, drunk on his scent. "Whatever the hell cologne this is, I approve," she said, flicking her tongue over the flattened disk of his nipple.

His body jerked, and he fisted his hand in the back of her hair. "Now it's my turn."

Crushing his mouth over hers, he released her hair and

slid his hands down her sides. Goose bumps sprung in their wake. And when his hands dipped lower, grasping the hem of her dress, a full body shiver racked her from head to toe.

This was actually happening.

He whisked the gown over her head.

Jason trailed the pads of his fingers along the red lace of her bra. A muscle clenched in his jaw. "So beautiful," he whispered.

Colby released a shaky breath, and Jason grabbed her hips, pinning her in place with his hands. They hadn't bothered with the lights when they fell into the room, so the soft lamp in the corner and the moonlight filtering through the plantation blinds were their only illumination. But under Jason's intent gaze, Colby suddenly felt as if he could see all the way to her soul.

It had been a long time since she'd stood like this in front of a man. A *very* long time. And now that she was, the only thing she could think about was all the pilates and aerobics classes she'd skipped over the years. She had curves. Breasts and hips, and an ass that was on the generous side of padded, thanks to her love affair with truffles and lasagna. Compared to Jason's chiseled body, did hers measure up?

Something in her face must have given away her thoughts because he shook his head. "Beautiful," he said again, this time with more force as he pulled her toward him. The lace of her bra grazed his chest and he hissed. "So *damn* beautiful."

Then his mouth descended, and any thoughts she held about her padded backside flew straight out of her head.

Scooping her up in his arms, Jason carried her to the huge bed, setting her down and climbing over her without breaking the passionate kiss. His tongue stroked deep in her mouth and she clutched the back of his head, demanding more. She wrapped her legs around his hips, and realized he still had his pants on.

"This won't do," she said when they broke for air. She felt his smile as his mouth trailed kisses along her collarbone. Yanking on his belt, she made quick work of the button and zipper then shoved at the fabric.

Jason chuckled and the sound zinged through her core. He palmed her calf, leaned up, and nipped her chin with his teeth. "I'll be right back."

What the what?

She didn't even attempt to hide her groan of frustration, which only made him chuckle again. He slid his wallet out from the seat of his pants, grabbed a silver square from inside, and tossed it on the night table. *Oh.* Then, dark eyes on hers, he pushed his pants and boxer briefs down over his hips and stepped out.

"So men really can look like that," she said, too stunned to be embarrassed that she'd once again spoken her thoughts aloud.

Jason exceeded every fantasy Colby had ever had. Long lean muscles. Curling dark hair. Washboard abs. And those mystical deep indentations above his hipbones. She pushed on to her knees and crooked a finger. "Come here."

He stayed in place, eyes raking over her, and she slid her bra straps off her shoulders. His mouth lifted in a grin, then opened as she reached around and flicked the clasp. Colby raised an eyebrow and repeated, "Come. Here."

Jason's throat muscles worked as he swallowed hard. "I—" His hoarse voice broke off and he cleared his throat. "I told you I had plans for dessert."

She tilted her head, watching as he zipped open his duffel bag. "I kinda thought we were in the middle of that plan right now."

Had she misread some kind of signal? You'd think

a situation like this would be pretty hard to misread but if anyone could misconstrue something like this, it would be her.

"Oh, we are," he confirmed, riffling through his bag. Relieved, Colby took a moment to admire his strong backside and sighed. Michelangelo's *David* had nothing on this man. "I just thought we'd take things up a notch," he continued, lifting what appeared to be a jar and a paintbrush.

She watched in confusion as he stalked toward her, holding the objects in his hands. He grinned and asked, "Ever used Chocolate Body Paint?"

Chapter Fourteen

Long after Colby fell asleep, his father's words kept Jason company. Shadows stretched across the floor as muted light crept through the blinds, and when dawn finally broke, and Jason looked down at the woman in his arms, he felt his world shift.

He was falling for Colby.

That truth didn't terrify him as much as he'd expected. Probably because he'd suspected it all along. But it did bring guilt. For so long, Jason had been content only loving one woman in his life. Ashleigh was irreplaceable. When she died, Emma became his entire world, as she should have. But after a night of holding this woman in his arms, Jason realized he now wanted more. Companionship and a wife with benefits weren't going to be enough for him. Would never have been enough with Colby. He wanted something *real*.

Why didn't that feel like cheating on Ashleigh's memory?

The vows he took may've said *till death do us part,* but the mother of his child deserved more than that. Or, so he thought. But after hours of torturing himself, the only thing troubling Jason's heart was wondering if Colby could ever love him back.

That might make him a bad husband, or maybe it was a healthy part of moving on. Either way, he was done guarding his heart. Colby broke through every line of defense he'd built up anyway. He wanted a lifetime of waking up with her in his arms, her long dark hair fanned across his chest. Of days spent laughing, teasing, and flirting. And nights spent just like the one before. Wrapping his hands around her sleeping body, Jason breathed in her floral perfume.

A soft sigh escaped Colby's silken lips. A smile touched his mouth as he lifted his head and glanced at the clock. Nine a.m. Colby had to be at the restaurant by eleven. With the thirty-minute drive back home and her having to get ready, it didn't leave them much time.

He pressed a kiss on the crown of her head. "Time to wake up, baby."

"Uh huh," she muttered, flinging her long leg around his hip. She crawled up his body, burrowed deeper into the crook of his arm, and buried her head against his neck. Morning person she wasn't.

Skimming his fingers down the notches of her spine and over the gentle curve of her backside, he lifted her higher, loving the feel of her tight body pressed along his. Colby sighed again, her warm breath fanning across his neck. "I guess we could just stay in bed all day. I'm not on shift; you can play hooky. We'll spend the whole day together."

Actually the more he thought about it, the more he liked the idea. He hadn't had enough of her yet. He doubted he ever would.

After a short pause, Colby's shoulders deflated. "Fridays are always crazy busy," she said drowsily, finally lifting her head. She pushed her dark waves away from her face, and the warm, satiated look in her gray eyes absolutely slayed him. "As incredible as your offer sounds, I have to go in."

"You sure I can't tempt you to stay?" He combed her hair to one side and dipped his head to the sensitive skin between her neck and shoulder. Last night he'd discovered kisses there had the power to put her in a very agreeable mood. "I'm sure there's a little more chocolate left in the jar—"

Scooting up, she slammed her mouth against his with a squeal. He chuckled, then proceeded to devour her, thrusting his tongue past her lips and spearing his fingers through her hair. Yep, the body paint had been an excellent idea. He grinned as his hands teased the surprising areas he'd uncovered thanks to the thick, sweet chocolate. Remembering how he'd licked and sucked it off her skin had a certain part of his anatomy jumping for round two.

Today, he was buying stock in the company.

"Shower," Colby declared after another minute, sinking her teeth into the lobe of his ear. "Now."

He groaned. "God, that feisty streak of yours turns me on." Her wicked grin said that was exactly what she was going for, and Jason slapped her ass as she leapt off the bed. "Consider me your love slave, woman. Your wish is my command."

"Hmm." She shoved aside her wild tangle of hair, and her smoky eyes darkened as she rimmed her top lip with her tongue. "The possibilities could be dangerous."

Shooting to his feet, he grasped her hips and yanked her against him. "Bring it on."

The joyous, playful sound of her giggle as he stole another kiss was like an electrical jolt to his heart. Damn, he really was falling for this woman.

Giving her space today to think was going to be hell, but it would be worth it. Colby needed to come to the same conclusions he had and he knew she had to do that alone.

Away from him. The thought that she could decide to push him away was terrifying. It made him want to latch on and drag her with him everywhere. But this was something she needed. And along with his daughter, Jason would always put Colby's needs ahead of his own.

She rubbed her nose against his, crinkling it as she smiled. "Ready to wash all that *sticky* chocolate off me now?"

He leaned back, giving her luscious curves a thorough examination. "I licked every inch of this skin last night," he said, watching the spark of desire flare in her eyes. "But, you can never be too meticulous about this sort of thing."

Seizing her shoulders, he spun her around and tugged her back so she could feel *exactly* how the image of her tight, soapy body affected him. Colby hissed a breath. She reached around to clutch his hip, and Jason grinned.

"Let's get you clean."

· · ·

The 985 was swarming with half-drunk women and overeager men, all looking to hook up. Colored lights streamed over bodies gyrating to a techno-remix of Taylor Swift singing about love. Colby pushed through a cloud of sweat, cologne, and stale cigarettes to one of the tables along the edge of the dance floor and plopped her exhausted butt on a stool.

Robicheaux's had been slammed, thus keeping the swarm of confusing thoughts and feelings banging around in her brain pleasantly at bay. When closing time came and Sherry suggested a girl's night, Colby had jumped at the idea, shoving her aching feet into a cute pair of boots. Tonight felt like a Tequila night.

Over the giant speaker to her right, the DJ's seductive voice coaxed the crowd. "All right, ladies, hope you're ready to shake it. For your line-dancing pleasure I've got Big & Rich's 'Fake I.D.'"

A shout of feminine *woots* preceded the scrape of chairs as a horde of women, and a few brave men, poured onto the dance floor. Colby glanced at Sherry with a mystified expression.

"It's from the new *Footloose*," she explained, her eager eyes following the crowd.

"I know you know this one," the D.J. continued as the music rolled in. "So come on out here and shake what your mama gave ya."

With the twang of the guitar and the pulse of the drum, cowboy boots began stomping in rhythm. Beside her, Sherry marked the time from her seat, shimmying and jostling the table until Colby gave her a good-natured shove. "Get on out there."

Her sister shook her head, but the excitement in her brown-eyed gaze gave her away. "I'm fine. I can totally hang here with you—"

"GO!"

Colby cringed. She never snapped at Sherry. It hadn't been her intention to do so now. All day her tension and confusion had been building, crackling under the surface. Messing with her during the lunch and dinner services. Causing her to make mistakes. And now she'd officially lost it. When she'd agreed to come out tonight, it was in search of a much needed distraction—not to have a freaking babysitter.

She forced a smile and tried again. "Go on," she said, more gently this time. She lifted her chin toward the clapping crowd. "Go show 'em how it's done."

Sherry's head tilted to the side and she shot a glance toward the dance floor. "If you're sure..." Colby nodded, and she flashed a grateful grin. "I shall return!" Then she scooted off the chair and the girl was gone.

Now it was time for Colby to get her drink on.

She waved at a waitress passing by their table. "Excuse me, can I get a margarita, please?"

"Sure thing, darlin'." The woman sent her an authentic smile from behind a pound of makeup. Grabbing an empty glass from the table beside them, she asked, "Frozen or on the rocks?"

"On the rocks." She deliberated and then said, "Better make that two."

The woman winked. "You got it."

Turning toward the crowded dance floor, Colby tried losing herself in the chaos. But as they had all day, her thoughts drifted right back to Jason.

Their night together had been amazing. But it proved what she'd feared all along—one night would *never* be enough. A summer with him wouldn't be long enough either. The glorious ache in her chest wasn't just some high from having sex again after the longest drought in history. The man had stolen her heart. And so had his daughter.

Last night she'd had a dream she was teaching Emma recipes in her childhood kitchen. Emma wore Colby's old checkered apron and the young girl called her *mom*. Colby didn't know the first thing about being a mother—yet, being with Emma was so natural. As much as the domesticated scene had rocked her, Colby had woken up surprisingly happy.

If Cane knew Colby was even considering staying in Magnolia Springs, he'd be thrilled. Well, after his reaction the other day, maybe not thrilled about the reason, but ecstatic about not having to hire another chef. Sherry would most likely begin planning their wedding. And Emma...well, it was obvious what that girl wanted. She wanted a family again. And if Colby stayed in town and began a *real* relationship with Jason that was exactly where they'd be headed.

But am I ready for that?

In her experience, fidelity was the stuff of fairy tales. But Jason's parents had somehow found a way to withstand the trials of marriage. So had her grandparents, and more aunts, uncles, and cousins than she could name. They all seemed to make it work. Maybe staying faithful wasn't just some mythical concept. Maybe her choosing a cheating boyfriend, after having been born to an unfaithful man, had simply been a case of severe, craptastically bad luck.

It was hopeful thoughts like these that had her tied in knots all day.

When Colby thought about the meaning of faithfulness, she thought about loyalty, trustworthiness, dependability, and consistency. Characteristics that Jason Landry not only had, but embodied. More so than any other man she had met.

Her choice was clear: believe in Jason and trust her heart, or let her past dictate her future.

She knew what she *wanted* to do. She just wasn't sure she had the courage.

"Fake I.D." ended and Sherry flounced back to the table, fanning herself with both hands. "Oh my God, that was fun!" She slid onto her chair and exhaled with a big old cheesy grin. "You should've come out there with me."

"What, and risk breaking an ankle? No thanks." The waitress set her drinks on the tabletop and Colby smiled her thanks. "Do you not remember what happens when I try to do coordination?"

Sherry stuck out her tongue then eyed Colby's drinks. "This one for me?"

She shook her head. "Nope. Get your own. I'm getting my drink on." Then she winked to show she was teasing and pushed the second glass toward her sister.

Sherry watched Colby take a sip of her cold, extremely yummy drink before taking a sip of her own. Smacking her lips at the tartness, she then leaned her chin on her hand. "So tell me, chica. Is this a celebratory get-your-drink-on, or a depressed one?"

Colby took another sip and shrugged. "I don't know. A little of both? Not ready to talk about it yet. Still too much swirling around in here." She twirled her finger over her head. "Distract me. Tell me about your love life. Are things going well with Waiter McHottie?"

"Ben?" Her voice took on that dreamy quality normally reserved for mint chocolate ice cream or candlelit bubble baths. "Things are better than good." Biting off a smile, she glanced down at the table. "This is gonna sound crazy, but I think he might be the *one*."

Margarita spewed out of Colby's mouth. Her sister may as well have declared she was thinking of becoming a nun. "Are you serious?"

A frown line appeared between her eyes as she peeled a wet napkin from Colby's second drink. Wiping at the table she said, "I know we've only gone out a couple times, but he's worked at the restaurant for a few months. It's not *that* crazy."

"No, I know," Colby said, her mind still reeling. "I—I just didn't realize things were like that between you."

Or that Sherry even believed in settling down. She was the wild child. The girl who had a new guy every week. The one who threw crazy parties on the weekends and loved defying social conventions. *Not* someone who believed in finding "the one."

"Everything is so different with him, Colby. Ben makes me laugh, and he's wicked smart. He's back in school to finish his degree, you know. He doesn't plan on waiting tables forever. And damn, the man is sexy as *hell*." She made a lip-smacking yummy noise and Colby laughed. *This* was the sister she knew. "I get goose pimples just thinking about him. And don't even get me started on his tongue."

When her eyes rolled back in her head, Colby interrupted. "Bordering on TMI, Sher."

Sherry giggled. "Prude," she teased, sitting up in her seat. "For real though, it's not like we've had 'the talk' yet or anything, but…yeah. Things are getting pretty serious."

Disbelief would be one way to classify her reaction. Shock would be another. They had been dating for like a second. Still, if her sister was happy, then she was happy. "That's great, Sher. Ben's a lucky guy."

She beamed. "Hey, maybe you and Jason can double with us next weekend. We can go see a movie or something."

And there went Colby's thoughts, straight back to the sexy fire captain. So much for her distraction.

Nodding, she picked up her drink. "Yeah, maybe." She took a long, extended sip and shook her head at the sharp punch of tequila. Coughing, she shoved away from the table and grabbed Sherry's hand. "You know what, though? You're right, tonight *does* feel like a dancing night."

Surprise lit her sister's eyes. "Really?"

"Yep," she said, popping her lips around the word. "Let's do this thing."

Out on the dance floor, Colby chased her distraction, grinding to the beat of "Country Girl." Her hands flew over her head. She tossed her hair and spun Sherry in a circle. Skimming her hands over her hips, she shook them like the lyrics directed. To her sister's delight, Colby broke into the Carlton, the Running Man, even the MC Hammer. She tried getting Sherry to do the Kid 'n' Play, but Sherry was too busy cracking up. Colby didn't mind—she was having fun. The few sips of her drink combined with the music had a warm tingle spreading across her skin and for the life of her, she couldn't remember why she'd hated dancing so much. The bar didn't have a mirror on the dance floor, which was a damn shame, but she was positive she looked absolutely *fabulous*.

Everywhere Colby looked, couples were dry humping themselves into oblivion. A particularly amorous man to her right had his date bent so far backward she felt voyeuristic sharing the same dance space.

She wiggled her eyebrows in the direction of the couple and screamed into Sherry's ear, "Guess we know who *she's* shaking it for tonight."

Her sister laughed. She moved behind them and made a half-obscene but completely humorous gesture, setting off another round of giggles. Yep, Colby was definitely feeling good.

The song ended and another began. She exhaled and closed her eyes, wishing Jason were there. If his performance last night was any indication, the man had moves. She could picture him slinging his arm around her waist, drawing her close as he swiveled those delectable hips. She smiled…then lost her balance as someone bumped her from behind. Eyes still closed, Colby threw her arms out in a blind lunge, and latched onto the couple playing tonsil hockey.

"I'm so sorry," she said as the man lifted his head, probably as much for air as from her groping him. "Some idiot —" She broke off as the two of them locked eyes. Colby froze, the happy vibes she'd been feeling instantly dissipating.

Oh, shit.

Chapter Fifteen

"How could I be so fucking *stupid*?"

Sherry's pained question came out as an accusation, and it broke Colby's heart. Handing over a hot bowl of gumbo, their mama's guaranteed cure for anything, she wanted nothing more than to drive right back to 985, rip the frizzy hair out of the other woman's head, and use it to string up Ben "the two-timing asshat" by the gonads. It had been years since she'd gone Mama Bear on anyone for hurting her little sister, but her claws were just as sharp as when they were kids. And after listening to Sherry cry for the last hour, she was itching to use them.

"You weren't stupid, Sherry. You trusted him. *He's* the jerk here."

Colby had been saying variations of the same thing ever since they left the club, but her sister still wasn't listening. She was fixated on the fact that Ben had claimed he had homework to do, and she'd believed him.

Evidently, *homework* was a skanky blonde with two-inch roots.

Sherry blew her nose and dropped another Kleenex in the

wastebasket. "I really thought things were different with him, you know? I thought we were getting serious. Either I was lying to myself or I'm an idiot, but either way, I'm pathetic." She yanked another tissue from the box and lifted her head. Biting her lip she asked, "Do you think she was prettier than I am?"

"Are you shitting me?" Her sister's mouth dropped at the profanity. Colby wasn't big on cursing, especially aloud, but if there was ever a good time for it, this was it. "Sher, you're freaking gorgeous. You're sexy and fun and have a heart bigger than Lake Pontchartrain. If Ben can't appreciate that, then you're better off. Trust me. That girl he was with tonight ain't got nothing on you, babe. It's his loss."

Sherry rolled her eyes as she dug her giant spoon into the steaming bowl. Stirring the thick stew until she had the perfect proportion of sausage, okra, rice, and broth, she mumbled, "Well, you're my sister, so you kinda have to say that."

Colby snorted. "No, as your sister I should hightail it to that club and go Lorena Bobbitt on his ass." She pulled back her sister's comforter and slid in beside her. "But then I'd be arrested, you'd be alone, and Robicheaux's would be without a head chef again. So instead, I'll stay here and just envision going chop happy. Besides, once Cane hears about this, Ben's gonna wish it'd been me playing fast and loose with a cleaver."

The spoon Sherry had lifted stopped in mid-air, her big brown eyes full of sudden panic. "Oh God, Cane's gonna go caveman on his ass, isn't he?" Colby nodded with glee, imagining the fierce, dark look she'd only seen a few times on her brother's face. Most days, he was like a giant teddy bear. A sarcastic, slightly arrogant teddy bear, but a teddy bear. But when it came to the people he loved, the man lived up to his bad boy looks and then some. Sherry shoved another heaping spoonful in her mouth, swallowed, and pushed the bowl back into Colby's hands. "I can't eat anymore. Can you save this for me?"

Colby's eyebrows furrowed as she set the barely touched bowl on the cluttered nightstand. "Sure, honey."

More than the dark smudges beneath her eyes, or the runny trails of mascara on her cheeks, her sister's unprecedented lack of appetite revealed how truly devastated she was. Colby wished the magic words would appear that could somehow make this right, or at least make it more bearable. But she guessed magic, like fairy tales, didn't really exist.

A small voice inside her head whispered, *See? You were right.*

Neither of them hungry, they sat together in silence for a long time, each lost in their own set of demons. The *drip* of Sherry's leaky faucet filled the quiet. Colby ran her fingers through her sister's multi-hued hair until eventually her swollen eyelids grew heavy. She waited until the sound of her breaths evened, and then she carefully slid from under the comforter.

Walking down the hallway to her own bedroom, Colby clutched her hands at her waist. The ruby ring her mother had left her sat heavy on her right hand. She twisted it and closed her eyes. Times like this, she really needed her mom.

They'd never spoken about her father's infidelity. Colby doubted she ever found out. The few times she'd come home over the years, her parents had always seemed happy—a lie that often infuriated her. If they were so happy together, then why did he have to cheat? He'd made her mother look like a fool, blindly trusting the man she'd loved.

Colby couldn't help but wonder: if her mother were still alive, what words of wisdom would she offer Sherry tonight? And if she knew the truth about her husband, would she honor that same advice?

Soft light from the bedside lamp spilled over Colby's cell phone and she picked it up. Sinking onto the mattress, her finger hesitated over Jason's name. She didn't know what she wanted to say. She didn't know what she wanted to hear. She only knew she had to speak with him. Remind herself that Jason wasn't Ben. That he wasn't her ex or her father. He was one of the good ones—the few good ones.

With a deep breath, she tapped his name.

Ring.

"Come on, Jason. Answer your phone."

Ring.

Her heart pounded as if her life depended on them speaking. If not her life, her sanity certainly did.

Ring.

Then, mercifully, his phone picked up.

"Oh, thank God. Jason, hey, I—"

You've reached Jason Landry, captain of the Magnolia Springs Fire Department. I'm sorry I missed your call...

Colby flung the phone across the bed, her eyes suddenly filling with tears. Anxiety rushed her veins. Her stupid stomach churned and clawed at itself. She was acting irrationally, she knew. Jason had done nothing wrong. Yet it was as if time reversed twelve years. Every doubt, every insecurity she'd felt back then had returned, fiercer than ever. She *had* to speak with him. There was no way in hell she'd get any rest tonight until she did.

It was only eleven. A perk of being the head chef expediting orders on the weekends. It was hellish and crazy, ensuring every dish was perfect and run to the tables efficiently, but it meant even on a slammed night she was often out by eight. Any other night she'd have gone home, put up her aching feet, and drank a half-bottle of wine in front of the television. Tonight, however, she'd managed to go clubbing, witness the destruction of her sister's love life, and watch her cry herself to sleep, all before *The Tonight Show* even came on.

Her world had tipped on its axis in a matter of hours. Somehow, that didn't seem possible. But it was.

Colby pushed to her feet and began pacing the length of her room. Her skin felt tight, like the ickiness of the night was trying to escape through her pores.

Where is he?

After another minute wondering, imagining every possible worst-case scenario, she grabbed her keys. Any trace of alcohol in her system from those few small sips had burned out long ago. Pocketing her phone, she marched back out into the hallway. Staying here would only make her stir-crazy. And wear a hole through the rented carpet. She checked on a still sleeping Sherry, jotted a quick note on the kitchen white board, and bolted to her car.

The first place she'd check would be the gym. It was closest to the house and she thought that maybe he had a class to teach. If his truck wasn't there, she'd drive by his house, then his parents', then the station.

Yep, she was in full-on stalker mode. She could admit it. But she *had* to see him.

Her first easy breath entered her lungs at the corner of Wisteria. Jason's truck sat parked below the sign for Northshore Combatives. Her hands shook on the wheel as she turned in beside him. Soon, she'd be back in his arms and the knot in her stomach would unfurl. The ghosts of her past would disappear and she'd slam the door again on all her doubts. Hopefully Emma was at a sleepover or at her grandparents', because right about now the only thought in Colby's head was dragging that man back to his house, tearing off his clothes, and forgetting this whole night ever happened.

As she walked purposefully toward the entrance, she was aware there were a few cars still in the parking lot. She wasn't sure how many, didn't really care. She was willing to stay as long as it took to close up, as long as she was with him. She yanked open the door, a blast of cold air hitting her in the face, and stopped in the middle of an empty room.

The front desk where she'd first met Emma was deserted. Colby glanced around, unsure of where to go next. The place was freaking huge. Muffled noises—people talking and the muted beat of music—came from somewhere, but in front of her loomed nothing but a sea of unused cardio equipment. She dug her phone back out, ready to try calling him again, when salvation came in the form of a sweaty man with a towel slung over his shoulders. He rounded the corner of the stairs and stooped to get a drink from the water fountain. Colby attacked.

"Excuse me," she called, aware as she marched over that her voice was bordering on frantic. "Do you know where I can find Jason Landry?"

The guy stood, wiping his mouth as his bright green eyes trailed down her body. "He's in one of the classes finishing upstairs." *Oh, thank God.* The clawing ache of the last half-hour was almost over. Relief flowed through her as he indicated the stairwell behind him with a tilt of his head. "But I'd be happy to offer *my* services for anything that you need." He jerked his chin up and winked.

Ew.

And grr.

Couldn't this dude see she was in a tizzy here? Did he really think *now* would be the best time to hit on her...and with a cheesy line no less?

Somehow, she refrained from visually cringing—the man did help her after all. And with eyes already trained on the stairs behind him, she even offered a thin-lipped smile. "Thanks, but I really just need Jason. It's kind of an emergency."

The way her body was starting to shake, that felt about right.

With a strange flutter in her belly, she dashed toward the stairs.

. . .

A good workout always got Jason's blood pumping. Two-plus hours of drills and intense groundwork left his body depleted and covered in sweat—but it was a natural high. If he couldn't spend time with Colby, this was where he wanted to be. Nothing beat the euphoria of leaving it all out on the mat. Pushing his body past its limits. And for another night, knowing he did his part to honor Ashleigh's memory.

A soft cough shocked the hell out of him. He'd thought he was alone. Capping his water bottle, he glanced back, surprised to find Angelle. "What's up?" he asked, grabbing his towel from the floor.

"I'm still not confident about escaping from the bottom," she said, bouncing on her toes. She reached up and yanked her ponytail. "Could you maybe, um, show me again?"

Jason wiped the sweat off his face and arms, considering the question. The woman was an enigma. Vulnerability was practically stamped on her forehead. Half the time she couldn't finish a sentence around him without stammering. Yet despite being the only woman in the class, she'd handled the drills he'd thrown them remarkably well. Watching her *shrimp* across the floor tonight, he could almost imagine Ashleigh there doing the same.

He wasn't an idiot. He knew Angelle had her own reasons

for joining the class. Her completely unrequited crush was becoming a hassle at work, and he'd done everything he could to let her down gently. But he rarely had female members take his class. They joined the gym for the cardio equipment, or signed up for aerobics. That class was great—hell, he'd hired the best—but this could offer so much more.

An idea came to him, and Jason smiled. "Sure," he said, tossing the towel into his bag. "But let's take it a step further. We can actually apply the same principles to sexual assault defense. I offer a seminar every few months based on something I got from Gracie Jiu-Jitsu, but the basics align with this class, too. Get down on the mat, I'll show you."

A blush stole across Angelle's pale skin as she sank to the ground. "Yes, sir."

He held back a sigh as he joined her. This woman certainly stretched him as an instructor. But if he could cut through her misguided attempts at flirtation and find a way to empower her, then it would all be worth it.

"In a real life assault," he began, "a predator has one objective: to control you. Your goal is to convince him he's done just that. If you can get him to relax his grip for one moment, you have a shot of escape. This class is about defense at all costs, and employing deception is a big part of that. Feigning surrender is a valuable tactic. So you're gonna learn it. Get in position."

Angelle's blush spread as she bent her knees and spread them apart. Jason glanced at the door. It was wishful thinking that Cane would suddenly appear, fresh from the shower in the locker room. This was something his friend would love to help with, but it looked as though Cane was taking his sweet-ass time—and this skill was important.

Sliding between her bent knees, Jason locked Angelle's hips between his elbows and slipped his hands around her shoulders. Pretending not to notice her sharp intake of breath, he instructed, "Now, try to shrimp out."

She gave a few halfhearted attempts. "I can't. I couldn't get it in class, either."

Her voice was winded. He hoped that at least a part of that was from her sense of fight or flight kicking in. That was what he loved about teaching. Giving people a chance to experience real-life scenarios in a safe environment...and hopefully learn lessons they'd never have to use.

"I outweigh you by a hundred pounds," he told her, sitting on his heels. "It's almost impossible for you to escape. But I couldn't do much in that position, either. To assault you, I'd need to back up a bit. I'm not going to do that, though, until I feel a shift in power." As Jason spoke, her eyes lowered to his mouth. Biting off a growl of frustration, he asked sharply, "So what's gonna make me loosen my grip, Angelle?"

Annoyance tightened her mouth. But when her gaze lifted, he could tell he'd gotten through to her. Her eyes narrowed in thought. "When you think I've given up?"

"You got it." At her pleased smile, he went on. "A predator waits until he feels you've given up the fight. That moment you realize he's in control and you stop defending yourself. You go limp, and he gains complete control. Does that make sense?"

She nodded, and Jason could feel the shift in the air. She was in student mode now, and he did a mental fist pump.

"If you're in a position you can't get out of, it's your job to convince the attacker that he's accomplished his mission," he said. "That the fight has left you. That it's okay for him to relax his grip and move on from subduing you to the actual assault. Most victims, when they truly believe all hope is lost, stop fighting, hoping it'll just end soon. You're going to pretend you've reached that point."

"How?"

"You tell him that you give up," Jason answered. "Say you'll do whatever he wants. You *pretend* to give him the power he craves by asking him not to hurt you, and you stop struggling. That's key, because if your actions don't match your words, he won't believe it."

Angelle's head tilted. Her gaze sharpened and her mouth scrunched. Avid curiosity replaced every trace of breathless coquettishness when she asked, "So I don't even try to hit him?"

"Oh hell yeah. You're gonna do some damage, you're just gonna wait until he believes you've given up, however long that takes. Once you feel the grip on your hips lessen, you shrimp out. You shove your foot against his hip and push away, increasing the distance, as you kick him in the face, hit, slap, do whatever you have to do to get free and get the hell out of there."

A spark lit her green eyes and he knew she was imagining herself doing just that. With a sense of pride welling in his chest, Jason let his words sink in for another moment, then he said, "Now I'm gonna lean down again, trying to pin you. I want you to do everything I said. Pretend this is a real life situation. Kick my ass," he added with a grin. "Are you ready?"

A fierce look of determination crossed her face. "Yes, sir."

Immediately, Jason clamped his hands around her shoulders. Below him, Angelle thrashed. She shoved and grunted, trying to free herself even though they both knew it was futile. Then, as discussed, her struggle started tapering off. She went limp in his arms. As the attacker, Jason looked into her eyes, sizing her up to see if the power shift was real.

In character, Angelle's eyes softened as she placed her hands on his shoulders. "Please, I'll do whatever you want. Just—"

"Oh my God!"

At the sound of Colby's voice, the lesson was forgotten. Jason pushed back on his heels, hungry to see her face. He'd been thinking about her all day. His hands had twitched, wanting to touch her. And here she was.

Damn, she looked good.

"Baby, what are you—"

"Don't you *dare* baby me," she spat, freezing inside the door. She thrust her fingers through her hair, and Jason stiffened. Her hands were shaking.

Jumping up, his feet ate the distance between them as his arms reached out to hold her. When she flinched from his touch, a cold prickle of apprehension wrapped around his neck. "Baby, what's wrong?"

"I said, don't *baby* me." Eyes wide, she looked at him as if she'd never seen him before. "You're just like all the rest of them, aren't you?"

He didn't understand. "What?" Her eyes flicked to the mat behind him, and a fist of fear sank in his gut. The confidence he'd held all week drained away.

"Colby, Angelle's one of my *students*," he explained, knowing even as he did that it made no difference. From the look in her eyes, it was clear she'd already made up her mind.

Her eyebrows lifted. "Angelle?" Nodding as if something suddenly made sense, she asked, "The girl you and Cane were talking about at the restaurant. The one who inspired that weird look between you?"

That *look* had been because Cane was interested in his recruit and Jason hadn't wanted to bring her up around Colby. In hindsight, maybe that had been a mistake. But before he could even begin to explain that, she said incredulously, "So my brother knows about you two?"

He laughed, but the sound was far from amused. Just this

morning he and Colby had made love. Twice. Then he'd given her the day without distraction so she could think. Every time he'd wanted to call, he had restrained himself. He had been so damn sure that after their night together, she'd realize that she was falling in love with him, too. That he'd call her during his shift tomorrow or pick her up on Monday and she'd be ready to start the rest of their lives.

But his plan had failed. Nothing he'd done the past few weeks had made a bit of difference. The fact that this situation could be completely innocent wasn't even a blip on her radar. She was too busy acting as though she'd walked in on them fucking on the floor.

"Yeah, Cane knows Angelle," he said. "He knows that she works at the station. That she's a *student* here. He is too, if you remember. He's even here now, somewhere. If that had been your brother on the ground, would you be freaking out?"

Colby glared, and Jason knew that wasn't fair. She'd been upfront about her hang-ups. And truth be told, if the situation were reversed, he wouldn't be thrilled either. But she was refusing to listen to reason.

A soft cough and movement had him turning back to Angelle. Honestly, he'd almost forgotten she was still there. She looked between them as she pushed to her feet, her face taut with guilt. "I-I'm so sorry," she stammered. "I didn't mean to cause you any problems. I didn't know."

"Didn't know what?" Colby asked. "That he had a girlfriend? He wouldn't tell you that now, would he? But don't worry, honey. He doesn't have one anymore."

The words were sharp, but her voice broke at the end, giving her away.

Fear glistened her eyes, and a tremble shook her voice. Colby was hurting. It had to mean she cared. Yet she was standing there, throwing away everything they'd built over a damn misunderstanding.

Jason knew if they had any chance of making this work, he had to put his own anger aside. Flexing his hands, he strove for calm as he said, "Colby, this isn't what you think. What you're imagining didn't happen. I'm not your dad. I'm not your ex. I'm an instructor in a class that just ended, and one of my students asked for help. We were going over a skill that I'd love to show *you*. That's all that's happening here."

The battle was evident in her expressive eyes. A part of her wanted to believe in him, wanted to believe in them. But when Angelle brushed past on her way to the door, the softness that he saw last night—the look in her eyes that he'd believed was love—faded. And the side that had decided years ago that all men were dogs won out.

Hesitating with her hand on her duffel bag, Angelle sent him an apologetic smile. It would be easy to be mad at her. He *wanted* to blame her. But he couldn't. The girl had a harmless crush. He should've set her straight as soon as her feelings were obvious, but he'd ignorantly thought it'd only make things more awkward. He'd always known she was never an honest threat to their relationship. But not confronting the issue led to this disaster.

Turned out it was Jason's fault after all.

Gripping the strap of her bag, Angelle spoke quietly. "He's telling you the truth." Colby bristled, and Angelle turned to look her in the eyes. "Woman to woman, I did go after him. I didn't know he was seeing someone—but I never asked. Jason never did anything inappropriate. He was only ever professional and kind."

Colby didn't reply. He hadn't expected her to. But he was grateful Angelle had tried.

"Jason is an amazing man," she continued. "I can't be the only one who sees that. Don't be a stubborn ass." With a final glance back at Jason, she left.

The room fell into silence.

"Colby, I…" He squeezed his temples with both hands, searching for the words to fix this.

"Contrary to popular belief, I'm not a complete ass." Colby sighed, her entire body seeming to deflate before him. "Stubborn maybe," she muttered with a long exhale. "But I'm not an idiot. I heard what you said. I heard *her*. And I admit it's possible that I misread…whatever that was."

For the first time since she'd walked into the gym, Jason felt hope. But then her glassy eyes lifted. "It doesn't change the fact that I'm broken."

Swift steps bought back the distance she'd put between them. Yanking Colby into his arms, heart pounding, he shook his head. "No, baby. You're not broken. You've been hurt; I get that. But if we're ever gonna work, you need to trust me. You believed the worst tonight because that's what you expected to see. But Colby, I promise you, I'm not that guy. I'm not going to hurt you."

A fat tear rolled down her smooth cheek. Another followed. As he swept them with his fingertips, her lips lifted into a small, trembling smile. But he felt her slipping away.

"No." Wrapping his arms tighter, he crushed her against him, his voice quaking with emotion. "Don't give up on us, Colby. Couples fight. We can come back from this."

Her eyes closed as she lowered her head to his chest, shaking it as if to say, *I don't think we can.*

Desperation clawed his insides, tightening his chest. He refused to lose her now. Grasping her chin between his thumb and forefinger, he lifted it and pressed his forehead against hers, praying she'd open her beautiful eyes. When she didn't, Jason went for broke. "Colby, I love you."

A sob shook her slender body. A matching one built in his

throat. She had to feel the same. They could fix this. It wasn't over.

Colby flattened her lips into a hard line and finally opened her eyes...and Jason saw his dreams for the future shatter.

Cupping his face in her hand she whispered, "I'm so sorry."

Chapter Sixteen

"That's amazing, sweetheart." Jason wedged the cell phone between his ear and shoulder, a smile forming at Emma's excited chatter. His head pounded from lack of sleep. He was restless after hours on shift with no calls, and his chest ached—though that had nothing to do with his job. But he had his daughter. She would always have him. Their family unit was back to two, and perhaps that was as it should be.

"Yep, I totally kicked his butt," she declared. "After the first hour, the fish just stopped biting for him. Pops said it's because I'm so sweet."

Jason suspected it was more like a combination of the old man's soft spot for his granddaughter and good old-fashioned trickery. But as Emma giggled in his ear, the sound like a balm to his dropkicked heart, he was grateful whatever the reason.

"Well, you be sure to stick it to him good for me." He plopped his feet on his desk, picking up the picture of them in Biloxi last summer. "Do you know that in all the trips he's dragged me on, I've never caught more than him?"

She *whooped* and began taunting both men gleefully. In the background, he heard his mom scream at her favorite soap opera. Everything sounded so...normal. Eyeing the clock, Jason counted the hours until he could go home.

Rubbing a circle over the pain in his chest he said, "How about a celebratory fish fry tomorrow when I get home?"

"Mmm, sounds yummy. Can Colby come, too?"

The sound of her name in his daughter's sweet voice nearly killed him. How in the hell did he answer that? He couldn't destroy Emma's hopes over the damn phone. He couldn't even imagine doing it in person. His greatest fear had come true, and there was no one to blame for the fallout but him.

Ever since Colby had walked back into his life, he'd encouraged Emma's matchmaking schemes. Maybe not overtly, but in small ways he'd allowed it to continue. He'd pushed Colby to join their camping trip when she hesitated. He'd let Emma invite her to the Recognition Assembly. And at the restaurant the other day, he'd practically worn a neon sign in front of God and everyone declaring his growing feelings.

Even though Jason had been wrong, even though Colby didn't love him, he knew she cared about his daughter. She wouldn't shut Emma out. But after proclaiming his love like a jackass, Jason wasn't sure *he* could handle being around Colby again.

"I don't know, Em," he told her, his voice tight. Clearing his throat, he went for a diversion. "But you can invite Molly and Ava over. Now that summer break has started, it won't be a school night. Y'all can have a sleepover."

It was a cheap trick. A pathetic attempt at distraction—but it worked like a charm. For the next few minutes, Emma went into passionate detail, describing all the movies they'd watch and the snacks he'd have to buy. Following the maze of words and topics kept Jason's mind occupied, and he decided right then and there that this would be the best damn sleepover in the history of sleepovers. After everything she'd been through in her young life, his daughter deserved it.

"Oh, and we'll need doughnuts," Emma said. "Dad, what do you think — "

A loud bell pierced the air. A red light flashed over his head. Jason shot to his feet.

Emma's sharp intake of breath hit his ear as a booming voice called for three engines, a ladder, and the medic. "Respond to a structure fire at Twenty-six Boudreaux Park west of Lafayette. Zone Five."

"Daddy?!?"

Fear coated Emma's voice. It was the same sound he awoke to whenever she'd had one of her nightmares. They weren't as frequent anymore, but dreams of losing him like she'd lost her mother still tortured her some nights. In their small town, the department rarely responded to more than nine hundred calls in a year. But every fire Jason went into spurred another dream for Emma.

Tucking the cell phone by his ear, he ran toward his gear. "Everything's gonna be fine, Bug. I have to go now, but I love you. So much."

Her loud sniff carried over the sound of his boots smacking the ground. "I love you, too, Daddy. Please, *please* be safe."

"Always," he promised.

In a matter of minutes, Jason was dressed and racing down Main Street. Pushing past the guilt of Emma's fear and the pain of Colby's rejection, he began preparing for the task ahead. Fires were messy. Every one he'd encountered was unique and unpredictable. But this was what he'd trained for. *This* was something he could handle. And he was ready.

. . .

"Colby?" Cane widened the door as he stepped back, motioning for her to come inside. Staring first at her wardrobe and then at the key in her hand, he raised an eyebrow and said, "I thought you were sick."

In a manner of speaking.

Colby doubted her big brother considered heartache a legitimate illness. Especially not self-inflicted heartache. But after tossing and turning all night and then berating herself for being a spineless coward all afternoon, she was fairly sure she was normal sick, too.

Padding inside the home of her childhood, she breathed in the familiar scent of lemon. "I just needed to be here."

Cane gave her a searching look and nodded.

She had been in a daze since dawn. After waking up alone, which was completely her own fault, she'd walked down the hallway with swollen eyes. She'd ruined her eggs and burned her toast. *What the hell kind of chef burns toast?* Her glass of fresh squeezed orange juice held no taste. Even her morning shot of caffeine did nothing to clear the static in her head. When her sad yet determined-to-recover sister got a good look at her, she'd sent Colby straight to bed, on strict orders to take the day off. Considering what she'd done to her breakfast, it was probably for the best.

But Colby never went back to sleep. She'd lain in bed, watching crap daytime television. She'd bawled at every Hallmark commercial. Chucked her pillow at the romantic love scenes. And after *Ellen*, she'd finally dragged her sorry ass out of bed. The adorably perky host had reunited a guest with her first love, and Colby couldn't take anymore. With the walls of Sherry's house closing in, she escaped to her car, still dressed in her faded cat pajamas. Then she headed here, to the house that had created the starry-eyed girl she used to be.

The girl she wished she still was.

Now, Colby's slippered feet carried her forward. Cane fell in step behind her, his heavy footfalls echoing on the hardwood. Butterflies swarmed her stomach and tears pricked her eyes when she reached her final destination. "It looks exactly the same."

The butcher-block island. Dark oak cabinets. And umpteen magnets on the fridge. Cast iron pots dangled from the ceiling, and the aged GET IT WHILE IT'S HOT sign hung over the sink.

They'd gathered here after their father's funeral, but even then, Colby hadn't lingered. In the years since she'd left, the handful of holidays she'd actually come home for, she'd made it a point to never stay in this room longer than was absolutely necessary.

Cane chuckled. "Did you expect me to knock it down the minute y'all signed it over to me? Dad would haunt my ass from the grave."

Skimming her hand along the granite countertop, Colby shrugged. "I don't know what I expected," she admitted, somehow feeling more lost than when she'd walked in. "For some reason I just felt like I had to be here." She glanced around, failing to see any mystical signs from her mom, and sighed. "Sounds pretty stupid now that I say it aloud."

Frustrated and exhausted, she leaned her back against the cabinets and stared at the mottled tile beneath her feet. Ever since she'd come home, her life had been a constant roller coaster. And she was ready to get off.

Every street corner held a memory. Restaurants in two different states depended on her. Her head chef Matt had earned his promotion twice over since she'd left Vegas, but it was still on her shoulders—along with her family's legacy. The man she'd fantasized about her entire life, the man she'd fallen head over heels in love with, had actually told her he loved her. And in response, she'd *apologized*.

Broken didn't even cover what she was.

"You okay, sis?"

Colby replied with a thin-lipped smile, blinking back tears that insisted on forming, and Cane gave her foot a pointed kick. "You sure about that?"

Remembering her appearance—cat pajamas, ratty slippers, messy ponytail, no makeup—she laughed, only it came out more like a garbled sob. "Not so much."

Before her next breath, her brother had her wrapped in his big, bulky arms. Burying her head in the rock wall of his chest, she let the tears flow.

He kissed the top of her head. "You know that whatever it is, you can talk to me, right?" She nodded but kept her face tucked against him. "I might not have breasts like Sherry, but I *do* have two functioning ears. And thanks to a houseful of women, I even know to shut up and not try and fix it."

Colby laughed through her blubbering. Wiping her eyes, she raised her head and said, "Yeah, I know."

He smiled. When she didn't follow that with a baring of her soul, he ran his hands up and down her arms. "You'll be okay here for a minute? I want to get you something."

"Sure," she said, catching the time on the microwave. "But don't you have to get back to the restaurant?" It was just after four-thirty, and Cane never showed up after five on a Saturday.

"The world won't end if I'm late once," he told her, already backing away. "There's something I need to give you. Don't go anywhere, all right?"

She nodded, her nose scrunched as he jogged from the

room. *Something he needs to give me.* She didn't have the faintest idea what it could be, but if it was money, she was going to deck him.

To keep herself from another ugly cry, Colby decided to spend the minutes digging through the drawers. Cane hadn't changed a thing since inheriting the house. The junk drawer still held a slew of crap best dumped in the trash, and the kitchen utensils remained mismatched and haphazard. For some reason, the familiarity made her smile. She lifted her head, chest feeling lighter than it had all day, and found herself staring at an apron hanging on the side of the fridge.

A *checkered* apron.

Her apron.

"Got it."

Her brother's voice at her ear caused Colby's heart to spasm. Spinning around, she slapped his bulging bicep. "You nearly gave me a heart attack, you freak."

"Not my fault you zoned out," he said with a grin. "I'd be shirking my sibling duty if I didn't take advantage."

"And we wouldn't want that," she replied, shifting her head to the left to steal another look at her apron.

Following her gaze, Cane lifted his chin. "You know that's been there since you left for New York."

Now that she was busted, Colby turned around to get a good look, wondering why she hadn't noticed it before. But then, she knew why. It was on the side of the fridge near Dad's special alcove, the spot he kept all his prized recipes and spices. During those few short visits home, if she did venture into the kitchen, she avoided *that* corner like it held the plague. "Oh."

"You know, Colby, I'm not blind," he said, shocking her attention back to him. Cane exhaled and ran his hand over his face. "I knew about the tension between you and Dad. And I have a pretty good idea why, too."

He slid a hunter green envelope from his pocket and held it out to her.

Colby's hand flinched at her side, but other than that, she was frozen. "Dad's stationery."

"I found this in Dad's desk a couple days ago." Her eyes flicked to his, and Cane shook his head. He retracted the eerie note from beyond and flipped it over, pointing to the front cover where her name was written in her father's tight scrawl. Shivers skated down her spine. "No, I didn't read it. I got my own letter."

"Did you read yours?"

He shook his head again. "But I can guess what's in it."

I bet you can't.

Cane held the envelope out again, and this time she took it. The tips of her fingers tingled as they touched the stiff paper. Shifting his feet, there was an apology in her brother's voice as he said, "We should have talked about this years ago."

Colby's hand tightened around the missive as fear, anger, and even hope mingled in her chest. Did he know about their father's secret—her secret? "Talked about what?"

Cane folded his arms and leaned his hips back against the butcher-block island. With a shake of his head he said, "At first, I really did think that school in New York and the job in Vegas were good things. You wanting to get out of Dad's shadow. Make a name for yourself. And damn girl, did you ever." The smile he gave her was full of pride, then, it turned to something else. "But after a few years of excuses and you never coming home, and a few more where you did and it was uncomfortable as hell, I realized you *knew*."

At that one word, and the emphasis he placed on it, Colby's knees gave out.

"Oh, God." She fell back against the counter, covering her mouth with a shaky hand. "You knew, too."

"Walked in at the end of a phone call where he was apparently ending it," Cane replied. "Of course, Dad denied it. But I knew what I'd heard and by that point, I'd already heard the rumors. The woman left town not too long after that, and he came to me full of apologies." Cane laughed once, and harsh. "I wanted nothing to do with it. I was furious. Beyond furious—I was *pissed.*"

Colby nodded, knowing exactly how he felt. Except, Cane had been spared the visual.

"But after a while," Cane continued, "I don't know, he was still my dad. Mom was happier than I'd seen her in years. I never heard another rumor. It's not like I ever forgot what he did—I'll never forget that." He shrugged his large shoulders. "But I guess I forgave him for being flawed."

She didn't have a response to that. Her brother sounded so...*healthy.* Here she was in cat pajamas and ratty slippers, throwing away the best thing that had ever walked into her life, and her brother was suddenly Dr. Phil.

"Does Sherry know, too?" she asked.

A muscle ticked in Cane's jaw. "No. Whenever she asked what I thought was going on with you, I played up how busy you were. I shielded her from everything with Dad. Until a few years ago, I'd thought I'd shielded *you.* Clearly, I failed. And once I figured out that you knew, I should've done something. Talked to you about it."

"And what would that have done?" she asked. "Cane, this was Dad's fault, not yours. It wasn't your job to protect me from his mistakes. And no amount of talking would make me *un*see what I saw."

"Maybe not," he conceded with a soft smile full of regret. "But you would've known you weren't alone."

Colby squeezed her eyes against his words. He was right about that. For so long she'd felt alone. Before that night at the campground, she hadn't told a single person about that horrific day. But with Jason, she had. And it felt good to know she could talk to her big bad brother, too.

She went on tiptoe and slung her arms around his neck. "Now I do know that," she told him, placing a soft peck on his cheek. "And you're not alone, either."

Cane wrapped his arms around her waist and hugged her tight. For a long moment, she stayed there. Letting him hold her, and holding him back. Sharing the hurt they'd had to shoulder on their own. When she sank back to her feet, they shared a look of relieved stress; then as one, their eyes fell to the envelope clenched in her hands.

What in the hell is in it?

"Should I read mine now?" she asked, quite honestly scared of the thing.

"If you want." He stepped away to give her privacy and checked the clock. "I'll stick around for a few more minutes in case you need me."

Colby tried for a brave smile, but he saw through it. Cane squeezed her shoulder on his way out of the room and she waited until he disappeared down the hall. Then, alone in her father's kitchen, she tore open the envelope.

There were actually two letters nestled inside—one in her mother's handwriting, the other in her father's. Halfway through the first, tears back in her eyes and cascading down her cheeks, Cane's annoying duck call ringtone broke the silence.

"Emma?"

Colby's head snapped up.

"Em, you gotta slow down. Where are you?"

He appeared in the door, keys in hand, and at the look on his face, Colby started to shake. Clenching the letters in her hands, she tried moving to join him. Her legs wouldn't respond.

"I'll meet you there," he said. "Yes, I'm bringing Colby." He lifted an eyebrow and she felt herself nod. "We'll be by your side before you know it. Everything's going to be okay, Em. Your dad's the toughest son of a bitch I've ever met, you hear me?"

Hanging up, Cane took three long strides and grabbed Colby's hands. Too scared to bother correcting him for his language—Emma had probably heard worse anyway—she asked, "What? What happened? Where are we going?"

"Northshore Hospital." He crushed her fingers in his grip. "Jason's been hurt."

Chapter Seventeen

Jason's been hurt. Colby repeated those three words so many times on their way to the hospital that they no longer held any meaning. Panic seared a hole in her chest as images flashed in her mind. He *had* to be okay.

From the passenger seat of Cane's truck, she watched the world fly by without seeing. "Emma didn't tell you anything?" she asked again. "Not a clue about how bad it is, or what happened?"

Her brother sped around a car daring to go the actual speed limit and tightened his grip on the wheel. "No. I don't think she knew. And I was trying to calm her down."

Colby closed her eyes, unable to imagine what Emma was going through. "Of course; you did the right thing. I'm glad she knew to call you."

Cane gave her a quick glance. "I think she was looking for you."

One never-ending mile later, the hospital loomed into sight. Cane careened around the right turn without slowing and gunned it toward the Emergency Room. Pockets of firefighters already lingered near the main doors, and Colby clutched her stomach as she rocked in her seat.

Would they be here if it weren't serious?

The moment Cane threw his truck into park their doors were open. As agreed, he headed straight to the front desk while she rushed to the waiting room, searching for Jason's family. Eyes wide, it didn't take long to spot the blond ponytail huddled near the windows. "Emma."

The young girl's head shot up from her grandmother's shoulder. "Colby!"

Pushing to her feet, Emma tore across the linoleum floor. Frozen in place, seeing Jason's mom in tears confirming this was real, Colby could only open her arms. The girl threw herself into them. Her tiny body was trembling, her big brown eyes pooled with fear. "I'm so scared," she whispered, almost as if she was afraid to admit the truth aloud. "I can't handle losing him, too."

Closing her eyes against the fresh stab of pain, Colby tucked Emma's head under her chin. "You won't, sweetheart." She swallowed hard and opened them, her gaze falling on his mother. "You *won't*."

Emma's skinny arms tightened around her waist as she began sobbing in earnest. Running a hand over the girl's ponytail, she leaned down and pressed her lips against the top of it. A new batch of tears pricked Colby's eyes. This girl owned her heart.

Blinking the moisture away, she hoarsely asked Sharon, "Have y'all heard anything?"

"Not much." His mother's lips tipped up in a quivery smile. "One of Robert's friends at the station called as soon as it happened, but all he said was to come here. Robert's finding out what he can." Glancing at her granddaughter in Colby's arms, her eyes filled with remorse. She lifted a rosary-wrapped hand to her mouth. "Emma heard him on the phone.

She refused to stay home. We didn't know what to do."

Colby nodded, understanding.

Keeping a firm grip around Emma, she walked them back to the empty chairs near Sharon. Hands interlocked, Emma squished beside her in one chair, and the three of them sat in silence, waiting. On the wall-mounted television, the five o'clock news began, and Colby's shoulders locked with dread. Would they show footage of the fire? Could she watch if they did?

Movement just outside the waiting room stole her attention. Her brother had stopped in the hallway; his dark head huddled with the Chief's. The man looked as though he'd aged ten years since she last saw him. And Cane's hair, which always defied grooming, stood on end more than normal. His jawline clenched and his gaze shifted to Colby. Time stopped.

"What did you hear?"

She hardly recognized the voice as her own, but somehow it carried over the squeak of soles and the pages over the intercom. The men exchanged a look, and then trudged forward.

Rigid lines etched both their foreheads. Cane's hands were buried deep in his pockets. Although she was sure they walked normally, it felt as if they moved in slow motion. When the men came to a stop in front of her, pinpricks of pain pierced the back of Colby's hand. She glanced down and saw the tips of Sharon's fingernails embedded in her skin.

"There was a backdraft in the attic," his father said with obvious reluctance, reaching out to stroke Emma's cheek. "The first-floor ceiling collapsed, and Jason was inside."

A wave of vertigo almost sent Colby to her knees.

"Debris struck him in the head and knocked off his mask," he continued. "Jason was unconscious when the crew found him, but he was awake before they left the scene, and he was moderately responsive." Looking each of them in the eye, he said, "That's a very good sign. We'll know more when they finish their tests."

At the man's optimistic smile, the vise-grip crushing Colby's chest lessened a fraction. Taking a shallow breath she asked, "Was anyone else hurt?"

Her brother ran his hand over his jaw. "The explosion picked up one of Jason's men and threw him into the street. Glass got him pretty good, and he fractured an ankle. The doctors are taking him back for tests just in case." Cane tilted his head, indicating a young woman seated two rows over who looked as scared and lost as they did. "That's Michael's wife."

A pulse of kinship passed between them as Colby locked eyes with the firefighter's wife.

Beside her, Emma squirmed. Wrapping her arms around her legs she asked, "How long until I can see Dad?"

Colby turned to the Chief, wanting to know the same thing.

"It's probably going to be a while, peanut." His bushy eyebrows drew together as he glanced at the clock on the wall. He sent Colby a weighted look and said, "But you know, I saw a McDonald's up the road. I'm sure you're getting hungry about now."

Colby got the message. "Really?" she asked, feigning enthusiasm. Honestly, the last thing she wanted to do was leave. Or eat. She wanted to stay right where she was, all night if she had to, until she saw Jason with her own eyes. But he wouldn't want his daughter sitting out here, waiting for hours, scared to death. Colby didn't want that either.

Taking the keys from Cane's outstretched hand, she nodded at Sharon's smile of gratitude. She pushed to her feet and said, "I could go for some fries about now. Maybe a Big Mac. What do you say, Em? Uncle Cane has my number.

He'll call the second they hear anything." Emma pinched her bottom lip between her fingers, and Colby tugged on her elbow. "You're not gonna make me eat by myself, are you?"

With a sigh, the girl set her feet on the floor and stood. "I guess not." Turning to Cane, she asked, "You'll call if you hear anything?"

He nodded. "Cross my heart."

As assured as she could be in this situation, Emma blew out a breath and took Colby's hand. They walked that way, hand in hand, through the exit doors and into the parking lot. Colby needed the connection just as much as Emma did.

When they reached Cane's truck, they clambered inside and buckled their seat belts seemingly on autopilot. Neither of them said a word. Colby didn't want to push. But as the engine rumbled to life, Emma turned in her seat. "Can I ask you a question?"

"Anything," she said without hesitation. Even if the truth was painful to admit, Emma deserved complete honesty. She'd been through so much in her short life. Steeling herself for an uncomfortable question, perhaps about how she'd broken her father's heart, she glanced over and found Emma's eyes shining with amusement. Her smile spread across her face, and despite everything, Colby found herself returning it. "What?"

Emma laughed. "Are you wearing pajamas?"

Hours later, still in her cat pajamas, Colby let herself into Jason's house. After stuffing their faces with fries, they'd returned to the hospital in time to stand over a sleeping captain. According to Cane, by the time the doctors allowed them back, Jason was awake long enough for his mom to see the color of his eyes, and then he was out again.

The official word from Jason's battery of tests and scans was smoke inhalation, bruised ribs, and a mild traumatic brain injury, which scared the crap out of Colby, but boiled down to them needing to keep him overnight for observation. If his next CT scan came back stable in the morning, he'd be free to go home.

She'd offered to stay with Emma for the night so the girl could sleep in her own bed. Jason's parents had thought she did it to give them a break, but truthfully, her motives were selfish. She needed to be with Emma. She needed to be surrounded by Jason's things. She wanted to go to sleep in one of his shirts, slip between his sheets, and cuddle with his pillow.

"I'm gonna go to bed," Emma said, plodding across the thick carpet. Seeing her dad in that hospital bed, even asleep, had eased her anxiety greatly. She turned and yawned, blinking heavy eyelids as she asked, "We get to see Dad at nine?"

"We'll be there when they open the doors," Colby promised. "Go get some sleep, sweetheart."

Emma nodded tiredly. "Night." She turned back and began shuffling to her room. "Love you."

The hole in Colby's chest filled as she said, "I love you, too." She listened for Emma's door to click shut before slamming her head against the back of the sofa. "Now why couldn't I say that to Jason?"

She dragged herself up and locked the front door with a sigh, then directed her feet toward the Landry Hallway of Frames. The night Emma had given her the tour seemed so long ago. So much had changed…and so little really had. Colby was still the woman in love with her childhood crush. And she was still holding on to the past with an iron fist, letting it screw everything else up.

The soft glow from the nightlight in the bathroom lit the hall. Colby ran her fingers over each frame as she passed, watching Emma's life unfold via picture. She stopped in front of the wedding photo that captured her imagination that first visit.

"You have a beautiful family, Ashleigh," she whispered. "I don't think anyone can fill your shoes. I know I certainly don't deserve the position. But you should know they are deeply loved." Patting the corner of the gilded frame, she opened the door to Jason's bedroom and stepped inside.

Colby had expected a feminine touch. He'd once shared this bedroom with his wife, and she hadn't figured him to be the type to change it. But this room was all Jason. A sleek, modern, king-sized bed dominated the space. His comforter was deep green and simple. Hardwood floors were beneath her feet, and on the walls, his diploma, a baby picture of Emma, and a group shot of the Magnolia Springs Fire Department. A set of dumbbells and sparring pads were in the corner, and on the nightstand, a jar of chocolate-covered body paint.

Heat filled Colby's cheeks, both at the memory and the realization that Emma could've seen it. She picked it up to stash it, then hesitated. With a glance at the closed door, she slowly turned the lid.

The smell was just as delicious, just as enticing, as the night at the hotel. Sliding her finger around the rim of the jar, Colby stole a taste as she climbed onto Jason's bed and lay back against the pillows. As she'd hoped, they smelled like him—cinnamon and soap. The combination mixed with chocolate made her lightheaded.

She'd almost lost Jason tonight.

The irony, of course, was that she'd lost him the night before. Jason had held her hand and chased away the ghosts of her past, and all he'd asked for in return was her trust. And she hadn't even given him that.

After sealing the lid on the jar, Colby reached into her purse and yanked out the letters Cane had given her. During their extended visit to McDonald's, she had finished the letter from her mother. Walking out of the bathroom stall in her cat pajamas blubbering had terrified the little girl washing her hands, but she couldn't help it. Reading her mother's words from beyond the grave had been a game changer. Because, as it turned out, Colby had been wrong.

Her mother *had* known about the affair. The letters were apparently part of an exercise they did for marriage counseling. Her mom wrote that her dad had confessed his infidelity and begged her for forgiveness. They'd begun married life again with a fresh slate, happier than ever before. In the letter, she said that the world was filled with beautifully imperfect souls deserving of love, and her father was one of them.

Those words had kick-started the waterworks.

But her mother's ending line was what triggered Colby's bathroom breakdown: *Don't be afraid to love, Colby-girl. Love never gives up.*

The last part came from her favorite bible verse. Every time one of them had tattled or complained about another, their mother's reply had always been to quote 1 Corinthians 13. And for Colby to read that verse after she *had* given up on the man she loved—a man who lay battered and bruised in a hospital bed a mile down the road—it had simply been too much. She hadn't had tears left to make it through the letter from her father.

But reading it now, alone in Jason's room, seemed more fitting anyway.

"Time to get up, sleepyhead!"

"Aarrrggghhh." Emma dove under her pillow, mumbling about happy morning people. It almost made Colby laugh, considering no one in the history of forever had applied that label to her before. But today was a new day. In more ways than one.

"I've got homemade beignets," she tempted, prodding Emma in the side with a spoon. "And they are scrumptious, if I do say so myself. We're bringing a batch to your dad, so come on, chica. Up, up, up!"

With that, Colby left the girl's room, giggling to herself. Apparently, all it took for her to be the rise-and-shine-with-a-smile type was a severe lack of sleep, a good old-fashioned sugar rush, and her entire life being overhauled.

Her talk with Cane, discovering the letters from her parents, and almost losing Jason, had put everything into perspective. She awoke this morning a new woman. Or at least one with a new mindset. She'd made mistakes in her life and she had regrets—too many to count—but her father had loved her. He'd kept her apron. In his letter, he apologized for not being her hero, and then said that even though she had failed to show it, he never once doubted that she loved him, too.

Colby couldn't change the past. But the future was a whole different story.

In Jason's room, she tucked her parents' now wrinkled letters inside her purse with a contented smile. She was going to be okay. And now that phase one of her plan to win Jason back was complete, there was only one thing to do before she went to get her man: decide on her wardrobe. Should she go with choice a) the totally fashionable, day-old cat pajamas, or choice b) something of Jason's?

She glanced in the mirror and nodded. *Jason's.*

Dressed in a MSFD t-shirt that smelled like his aftershave and a pair of workout shorts rolled about a bazillion times, she emerged from Jason's room to greet a yawning, shuffling Emma. "Morning, sunshine."

The girl rubbed her eyes and shot Colby a look as they padded into the kitchen. "You're two seconds away from humming a show tune, aren't you?"

Colby laughed as she loaded a plate with beignets, dusted them a second time with powdered sugar, and slid the plate across the island. "I shall attempt to contain the perkiness while you eat," she said with a wink.

"That's all I ask," Emma replied, taking a huge bite of a fried doughnut.

As Jason's daughter made yummy noises, Colby set to work cleaning the mess she'd made that morning. Then she packed the rest of the beignets for the hospital. She knew it might be too late. Jason could have decided she was a head case after all and he was better off without her. But she wasn't leaving that hospital room until she'd put herself out there and, for once in her life, put her heart on the line.

At exactly ten past nine, their time slightly delayed by traffic, Colby and Emma walked back through the sliding door to Northshore Hospital. Her ratty slippers glided over the smooth linoleum as they made their way to the elevator. She was sure she looked a mess, but Jason had witnessed every one of her awkward stages growing up and had even seen her naked. A mismatched wardrobe was the least of her concerns today.

When they reached his floor, Colby's heart began to pound. Two doors down, she lost feeling to her feet. And just outside his door, she forgot the pretty speech she'd spent all night rehearsing. Emma scrunched her nose as she curled her hand around the handle. "You're coming in, right?"

Hugging the bag containing her peace offering, she nodded. "Most definitely."

This time when they walked into his room, Jason was awake. And he wasn't alone. Sharon and the Chief were seated along the left side of the bed, apparently *not* having fallen victim to the traffic. Colby's nervous stomach flipped. But then she got a good look at her captain, and suddenly she could care less if the whole hospital wanted to listen in on her groveling. Lying above the covers in track pants and a t-shirt, hair damp from a shower and feet wonderfully bare, Jason looked good enough to eat. And when he halted his channel-flipping to stare at her in obvious surprise, eyes raking over her body draped in his clothes, Colby half-wished she'd brought the jar of chocolate body paint from the nightstand.

"Daddy!"

Emma ran to the side of his bed, and Jason blinked as he shifted his attention to his daughter. "Bug!" He raised an arm slowly and said, "Be gentle. A house kicked your old man's butt yesterday, but I desperately need a hug from my girl."

Easing a knee onto the bed, she crawled beside him. He put his arm around her and closed his eyes tight. "I love you so much, Emma. I'm so sorry."

Sharon grasped her husband's hand and placed her other on Emma's head.

Colby's chest squeezed watching their four-way embrace. This was her family. Her second family. And she no longer felt like she was intruding or giving anyone the wrong idea by being there. This was where she belonged.

Emma sniffed into Jason's neck. "I was so scared."

"I know, baby." He opened his eyes and looked at Colby. "But it would take a lot more than that to take me away from you."

Hoping with everything in her that Jason was giving her

an opening, Colby took a step forward and held up the bag. With only a quick glance at his parents she said, "We brought breakfast."

The whole Landry family smiled at her, though the one from the man in the bed was closer to a wicked smirk. He lifted an eyebrow in question, and she took another step toward the bed.

"I come bearing bribery," she said, her voice wobbling but determined. "But homemade beignets are just the first phase of my master plan. The second phase is letting you know I've decided to stay in Magnolia Springs."

At the revelation, Jason's mouth fell open. She smiled as she took the third and final step. Things still needed to be ironed out, both here and in Vegas, and she had several phone calls left to make, but she knew what she wanted. She set the bag of beignets on the bed beside Emma, biting back a laugh. It looked like she was the one doing the surprising today. Remembering the outcomes of Jason's surprises—the blindfolded meal and their amazing night in New Orleans— gave her faith that this one would have a happy ending, too.

"The third phase is the most important," she said, crawling in on his other side, careful not to jostle. Sharon caught her eye over her son's head and smiled in encouragement. *Wow, this is embarrassing.* Smiling through the awkwardness, Colby forged ahead, looking only at Jason. "And that's making sure you know how completely, hopelessly, and unalterably in love with you I am. The both of you," she added, grabbing Emma's hand and ignoring the happy noises from her audience.

"I have made so many mistakes," she admitted, "and I've been terrified to open my heart. But Jason, it's *always* been yours. I've loved you ever since I can remember, and I will gladly spend the rest of my life making up for not telling you that sooner." She cupped his cheek with her free hand, desperately wanting to erase the memory of the night in his gym when she'd done the same—the night she'd almost lost everything. "I love you, Jason Landry."

For a moment, he just lay there, staring into her eyes. It had to be the longest moment ever recorded. But then he placed his hand over hers and the light she feared she had snuffed out came back into Jason's eyes. Colby began to hope.

And then, a nurse came in the door.

"I'm sorry, but Mr. Landry needs his final CT scan now."

Colby blinked her eyes.

Seriously? This couldn't wait, like, five seconds? The woman who Colby was almost certain was pleasant enough when she *wasn't* interrupting life-altering moments continued into the room, rolling a wheelchair. Colby looked to Jason, unsure of how to proceed, hoping he'd step in and ask for a few minutes of privacy—and discovered he had the audacity to be fighting back a smile.

"I really should do this now," he told her, making a move to scoot toward the edge of the bed. Colby stood, dazed and utterly confused. Gingerly, Jason pushed to a sitting position and took her hand in his. When he looked into her eyes, she noticed his were shining with an emotion she couldn't name. "This could be a while, so why don't you go to the restaurant and I'll come by there as soon as I get released. We need to talk."

Uh, yeah we do. "What about Emma?"

"We can take her home, dear," Sharon said, offering a smile though she looked as bewildered as Colby felt. The Chief, however, seemed to be in on Jason's private joke because his whiskers were twitching.

Now Colby felt like she was intruding. Had she really waited too long?

Picking up the purse she didn't even remember discarding,

Colby padded to the door, stopping just outside it to turn around. "See you later?"

Jason met her gaze. "I promise."

In those two words, Colby felt there was some sort of message. A message she wasn't getting. But she nodded anyway, and continued padding down the hall, back to the elevator.

What in the heck just happened?

Hours later, Colby was in the kitchen of Robicheaux's, just as confused as when she left the hospital, except now she was less dazed and more depressed. Jason never called. He never came by. She really had lost him.

It seemed her career as the future cat lady was trucking along right on schedule.

"Hey *Coley*, can you help me roll silver?"

Biting back a sigh, Colby tore her gaze away from her silent phone. If her sister was evoking her nickname and asking for help on a mindless task—an *unnecessary* mindless task, since Colby knew for a fact the silver was well stocked— the situation must be as bad as she'd thought. It was a good thing she hadn't called her head chef Matt yet, because it looked like she wouldn't be staying after all.

"Why not?" she replied. Rhonda and the rest of her staff could hold down the fort for a few minutes. Mindlessness sounded pretty good right about now.

Following Sherry into the dining room, Colby couldn't help scouting the faces, hoping to see *his*. Even though it had been a long shot, her shoulders still deflated. Her sister wrapped an arm around her waist and said, "Don't worry, girl.

I'm sure Jason just got caught up with Emma. He'll be here soon. I know it." She pulsed a squeeze and gave Colby an optimistic smile.

Colby returned it, although her hopes were sagging around her ankles. "You're right," she said, stopping next to the rolling station. "That's probably all it is."

Sherry grabbed four sets of silver and tapped Colby on the shoulder. "Now get to work, lazy bones," she teased. She scooted off to man more tables and the second Colby was alone again, her worried frown made its reappearance. Lazy was the opposite of what she was. Since leaving the hospital that morning, Colby had changed into her own clothes, washed a load of laundry, scoured the kitchen sink, inventoried the walk-in, and even cleaned the bathrooms. She'd just completed her *second* impressive pyramid of silver when the wail of a siren came from outside.

Like, right outside.

Concerned murmurs broke out as the patrons closest to the windows stood from their tables. The sound grew louder, closer, and more customers joined them, blocking Colby's line of sight.

"Did something happen to the building across the street?" she asked aloud, worried about the historic Southern style home, but her question was lost in the excited chatter. The wail seemed to come to a stop just outside Robicheaux's and Colby bolted to see what was happening.

"Excuse me," she said, politely shouldering her way past customers gathered near the front of the restaurant. Cane stood head and shoulders above everyone else near the main door and she raised her voice to ask, "Cane, can you see what's happening?"

Flashing red lights highlighted his wide grin, dimple in full view—an odd reaction to an emergency, she thought, but maybe it wasn't as bad as she'd thought. But then he grew serious, wiping any trace of amusement from his face. "You better come with me, Colby. I think you'll want to see this."

The solemnness of his voice paired with the intense look in his eyes got Colby's feet moving double-time. More than a few of the customers grinned in her direction, another weird reaction, and when she reached Cane she asked, "What on earth's going—"

He yanked her outside the door.

"—on?" Colby blinked, unable to process what she was seeing.

A fire truck was indeed parked in their lot. The siren had been silenced, but red lights still flashed. A semi-circle of fire fighters dressed in uniform stretched on either side, joined by handfuls of familiar civilians. But they weren't fighting a fire. They were just standing there, smiling.

That was enough to put the wrinkle of confusion on her forehead, but it wasn't what had Colby blinking her eyes like a crazy-eyed chica. No, *that* was due to the highly adorable, brightly colored, handmade banner attached to the ladder on the truck that said: *Will You Marry Us???*

Colby's jaw gaped open. She was definitely dreaming.

As if to prove that this wasn't some wonderful stirring of her imagination, Sherry suddenly appeared by her side, latching onto her right hand. Cane grabbed the left.

Colby looked up at her big brother with a question in her eyes, and he smiled.

"I was worried you'd both get hurt," he explained, referring to his obvious prior objections. "I see now I was wrong." When Colby mock-gasped in shock, Cane shrugged. "What can I say? Even *I'm* wrong from time to time. Guess no one's completely perfect."

Sherry snorted. "Lord, it's getting deep out here."

Cane chuckled and ducked down to press a kiss on the top of Colby's head. "Make each other happy," he whispered.

Awed, Colby nodded and looked out at the wide arc of friendly faces. If her hands weren't otherwise occupied, she'd pinch herself to prove this was happening. Sharon and the Chief were front and center in the pack, Jason's dad smiling and his mom dabbing at her eyes. To her right was old Mrs. Thibodeaux, who for an old lady seemed to pop up everywhere in Magnolia Springs. Jake from Jake's Seafood, Missy from LeJeune's bakery, and Tootsie from Trosclair's Convenience store were all there, too. It was like a strange, Cajun version of *The Wizard of Oz*. Of course, the arc was mainly made up of fire fighters, a few of whom Colby recognized from Taste the Heat and the hospital yesterday. And then there was Angelle.

When Colby locked eyes with the young woman, she seemed to shrink into herself. The redhead looked to the ground and bit her lip, then raised her head and met her gaze again with a small, hopeful smile. Without hesitation, Colby returned it. Nothing that happened that night at the gym had been Angelle's fault. The blame lay totally on Colby. She mouthed the words *thank you,* and relief crossed Angelle's beautiful face. The woman's smile widened as her eyes darted to the homemade sign.

Butterflies burst into flight in Colby's gut.

But where were Jason and Emma?

Whispers and cheers went up, and then the line of fire fighters broke. Colby watched, her heart in her throat, as Jason and Emma stepped forward. Just like the others, the man she loved was dressed in uniform, and he looked so good tears instantly filled her eyes. He confidently strode across the gravel lot, not stopping until he stood before her. And after sharing a wordless look with a beaming Emma, Jason sank to one knee.

Colby's breathing faltered. It was quite possible she'd forgotten how to perform the involuntary action altogether.

She'd been wrong before. She *was* dreaming. There was no way this was really happening. Any minute her annoying alarm would go off, yanking her from this wonderful fantasy. But until that happened, Colby wanted to soak in every moment.

Jason's lips turned up in that signature sexy, lopsided grin she loved. He lifted his chin at his best friend, and Cane squeezed his sister's fingers. Then Jason simply stared into her eyes and said, "Marry me."

Emma squealed. So did Sherry. Cane chuckled as his godchild bounced up and down on her toes chanting, "Say yes, say yes, say yes!" while Colby stood there like a blubbering idiot, laughing in amazement as she realized that what she'd *thought* she heard, what she'd dreamed of hearing ever since she was a little girl, had actually just happened. "Oh my God."

Happy tears sprang forth, falling freely down her cheeks as she released her siblings' hands and sank down to her knees. She pressed her lips to his, love, peace, and contentment filling her heart until she thought it would burst. This was her family. This was her *life*. And she was never letting go.

Leaning back, Colby rested her forehead against his, losing herself in the love shining in Jason's eyes. "Captain, I thought you'd never ask."

Welcome to Robicheaux's

Emma's Kicked Up Chicken Strips
Colby's Crawfish Beignets
Jason's That's How It's Done Crawfish Étouffée
Cane's Bacon Stuffed Jalapeno Hush Puppies
Sherry's Fried Catfish Sliders
Bite Ya Back Alligator Meatballs
Shrimp and Grits and Andouille, Oh My!
Just a Hint of Spicy Shrimp Quesadillas
Luxurious Lobster Mac and Cheese
Mini Muffulettas of Awesome
Oh That's Good Tasso and Boudin Jambalaya
Crawfish Pie a la Yum
Yeah That's Hot Cajun-Spiced Wings
Crab Cake Robicheaux
Not Your Mama's Fried Catfish
Who Dat Blackened Gold Chicken
Dahlin' Gimme Some Shrimp Creole
Fixin' to Eat Merliton Stuffed Bell Pepper
Lick Ya Lips Artichoke Dip
Stick to Ya Hips Deep Fried Cauliflower

Desserts

Bourbon Street Bananas Foster
Heavy on the Rum Bread Pudding
Big EZ Pecan Pie
Sinfully Delicious Doberge Cake
Gramma Robicheaux's Praline Cheesecake

Dear Reader,

Are you hungry yet? I feel like this entire series should come with the warning, Caution: Read with Snacks Nearby. Don't worry, for this special print edition, I've included four delicious recipes to feed your Cajun craving.

See, I love food. It's impossible not to be a foodie when you grow up in New Orleans. From seafood boils and barbeques, to red beans Mondays and fish fry Fridays, every party, event, and family gathering I attended growing up centered on one objective: celebrating life via yumminess.

Magnolia Springs may be a fictional town, but I based it on very real places. In Nawlins, everyone's a character, and the ones you've met and will continue to meet in the series have roots in people I know. My goal writing the Love and Games series is to bring a taste of my hometown's culture to you.

Where I come, we tease as fiercely as we love. We bleed black and gold for our beloved Saints and we cling tight to our superstitions. We beg and fight over cheap plastic beads, deep fry and sugar coat our treats, and share a faith that's deeper than I've found anywhere else. That's what I hope I've captured in these pages.

Taste the Heat is not just Colby and Jason's story. It's a love letter to the people of New Orleans.

Over the years, Hollywood has certainly provided comedic fodder about my hometown, but rarely do they capture the strong family bonds and the deep-rooted love for community that makes up our lives. History is made and life is shared around our meals, and what better way for me to show that— and take it up a notch—than feature a trio of siblings who own a Cajun Restaurant.

I hope you enjoyed Colby and Jason's story, and I hope you fall for Cane and Angelle in Seven Day Fiancé. Soon, wild child will Sherry meet her match, and I can promise you, it takes a special type of man to tame her. It may just be my favorite of the series!

Thank you so much for reading! I'd love to hear from you, especially if you try one of the yummy recipes that follow.

Bon appetit!

Rachel

Colby's Crawfish Beignets

INGREDIENTS
Beignets:
- 2 quarts vegetable oil for deep-frying
- 2 eggs
- Optional: Louisiana Hot Sauce
- 6 ounces crawfish tail meat
- 1 tablespoon creole seasoning—preference Tony Chachere's (plus extra for sprinkling)
- 1 teaspoon creole seasoning
- ¼ cup green bell pepper, finely-chopped
- ¼ cup green onion, finely-chopped
- 1 tablespoon garlic, minced
- 1 teaspoon salt
- 1 ½ cups flour, sifted (plus extra for rolling)
- 1 teaspoon baking powder
- ½ cup milk

Sauce:
- ¾ cup mayonnaise
- ½ cup ketchup
- ¼ teaspoon Louisiana Hot Sauce
- Optional: ¼ teaspoon prepared horseradish

DIRECTIONS:
1) Heat oil in a deep-fryer over medium-high heat to 365 degrees F
2) Whisk eggs in a large bowl until frothy. *option: add a dash of hot sauce to the eggs for extra kick

3) Sprinkle crawfish tails with 1 tablespoon creole seasoning and add to eggs

4) Stir in bell pepper, green onion, garlic, salt, flour, baking powder, and milk. The mixture will be thick and wet.

5) Using a large metal tablespoon, scoop and drop the beignet mixture into the hot oil a few at a time, and fry about 3 minutes or until crispy and golden brown on both sides. Do this in two batches.

6) With a slotted spoon, remove beignets from the oil and drain on paper towels.

7) Sprinkle remaining 1 teaspoon creole seasoning over beignets when still slightly wet

8) In small bowl, combine mayonnaise, ketchup, hot sauce, and horseradish if desired.

9) Spoon sauce onto 4 dinner plates and place 5 to 6 beignets on top.

10) Sprinkle rims of each with reserve creole seasoning for garnish and flare.

11) ENJOY!

Emma's Kicked Up Chicken Strips

INGREDIENTS
- 6 cups Canola oil for frying
- 3-4 pounds of boneless, skinless chicken breasts, cut into ½ in strips
- 3 eggs
- 2 tablespoons white pepper
- 1 teaspoon creole seasoning
- 2/3 cup all-purpose flour
- 2 teaspoons paprika
- 1 tablespoon salt
- Optional: dash of Louisiana Hot Sauce

DIRECTIONS:

1) In a large re-sealable plastic bag, combine flour, white pepper, creole seasoning, salt, and paprika.

2) Break the eggs into a small bowl, add optional dash of hot sauce, and beat until well belnded.

3) Dip each strip of chicken into the blended egg mixture, and then drop into the plastic bag. Work in batches, adding chicken, sealing bag, and shaking to coat with the flour mixture. After each batch, place the coated chicken onto a rack to let dry. Drying allows for even browning on the chicken.

4) In an electric deep fryer or large, heavy skillet, heat oil over medium-high heat until the oil is very hot. Place the chicken pieces in the hot oil, one piece at a time. Leave enough space among the pieces to prevent crowding.

5) Cook over medium heat, turning until all sides are golden brown and meat cooked thoroughly. Roughly 8-10 minutes, or until the juices run clear.

6) Drain on a paper towel

Jason's That's How It's Done Crawfish Etouffe * Easy Prep Version*

INGREDIENTS

- 1 pound peeled crawfish tails
- 1 stick margarine
- 1 medium onion, chopped
- ½ cup bell pepper, chopped
- 1 cup celery, chopped
- 2 cloves garlic, minced
- 2 bay leaves
- 2 cups water
- 1 tablespoon Worcestershire sauce
- 1 tablespoon flour
- 2 tablespoons chopped green onions
- 1 tablespoon finely chopped parsley
- Pinch of cayenne
- 1 teaspoon salt

DIRECTIONS:

1) Melt butter in large saute pan over medium high heat. Add onions, celery, and bell peppers and saute until wilted, about 10 to 12 minutes.

2) Add crawfish tails, garlic, Worcestershire sauce, and bay leaves to the mix and reduce heat to medium. Cook for another 10 to 12 minutes, stirring occasionally.

3) In bowl, dissolve flour in water, and add to mixture.

4) Season dish with cayenne and salt. Stir for about 4 minutes, until mixture thickens.

5) Stir in parsley and green onions, cook for another 2 minutes.

6) Serve over steamed rice.

Bourbon Street Bananas Foster *Home Cook Version*

INGREDIENTS
- 1 pint favorite brand of vanilla or coffee flavored ice cream
- 4 small bananas, firm but ripe
- 2 tablespoons butter
- 2 tablespoons brown sugar, firmly packed
- cinnamon
- ¼ teaspoon banana (or other) liqueur
- ½ cup dark rum

DIRECTIONS:
1) Place 1 scoop of ice cream in 4 large, heatproof dessert bowls or glasses. Freeze until serving time
2) Peel and slice bananas.
3) Melt butter in saucepan and saute bananas until golden
4) Sprinkle with brown sugar and cinnamon
5) Ready to serve? Add liqueur and rum to banana mixture.
6) Light carefully. When aflame, ladle over frozen ice cream
7) Savor

Acknowledgments

I get teary-eyed whenever I get to this part. It takes *so* many people to bring a book to life, and often the little things mean the most. First and foremost, I have to thank my family. My husband, Gregg, is my rock. He helps me plot, he brainstorms titles, he reads every book I write, and he even critiques my writing—especially the dude conversations! He gets me hotel rooms when I really need a quiet space to write and takes care of the girls when I leave for yet another conference. Most of all, he believes in me. And it is because of him that I know what true romance looks like.

My two beautiful girls, Jordan and Cali, are by far my biggest fans. They tell everyone they know—and I do mean everyone—about my books. They love giving me plot suggestions, and while I may not take many of them, their enthusiasm inspires me and keeps me going. This book was actually inspired from an episode of *Chopped* we watched as a family, and our hobby of cooking together formed the basis of Jason's relationship with Emma.

Next, I have to thank the Greater New Orleans area. I was blessed to grow up in Jefferson Parish (on the Best Bank—

locals will get that), and though I've moved a few times over the last ten years, I wanted to write a love letter to the place I'll always call home. Good food, amazing people, unique music, and a culture that embraces history and tradition, nowhere beats Nawlins. I look forward to showing the world even more about our section of the world in the next two books!

My godmother, Rhonda Armantrout, went WAY above and beyond in helping me research this book. Her knowledge of every facet of the restaurant industry was a godsend—and if you notice, I totally used her name for Colby's fabulous sous-chef. Thank you for the pages and pages of notes and willingness to answer any question, even the silly ones, and for connecting me with a local firefighter to help with Jason's story. He'd rather not be named but I hope he knows what a blessing he was. Our conversation totally changed the ending of this book!

As I always say, my critique partners are my sanity. Without Trisha Wolfe and Shannon Duffy, I don't think I'd ever get a book finished. They push me, challenge me, encourage me, and inspire me. They were joined for this book by Tara Fuller and Cindi Madsen, who I KNOW I drove batty with e-mails. Tara, thank you for being the world's best beta reader on this, and Cindi, thank you for the cover quote, the phone calls, and the responses to questions sent at the most random of times. I owe all four of you like a tub of chocolate.

Karen Erickson, thank you for all your guidance and fun e-mails. You know how to make me laugh, girl. Rose Garcia, Lisa Burstein, and Diane Alberts, thanks for always being there to answer questions or give advice. Amber Troyer, thanks for reading the first half of this book and for supporting *everything* I do. And a huge thanks to the ladies of West Houston RWA for teaching me so much over the last two years—looking forward to many more!

Joey Thomas, of the Joey Thomas Band, thanks for letting me use your name. Emma's not your only fan around these parts. You are so gifted and we believe BIG things are in store for you!

Kelly P. Simmon of InkSlinger PR has taught me SO much in such a short time. She also happens to be one of the kindest, most genuine women you'll ever meet, and is an angel to have in your corner. Speaking of angels in my corner, I also have Tara Gonzalez, my literary cheerleader, and Heather Riccio, my ninja goddess. Seriously, these ladies ROCK!! A huge shout out to Jessica Turner and Misa Ramirez, for all the amazing things you do. Much love, ladies.

Stacy Cantor Abrams is like my fairy godmother. She plucked my YA debut out of the pile, believed in it and loved on it, and then believed and loved on ME. She never doubted that I could take my brand of humor and romance to the adult romance world, and that unshakable faith gave me confidence. If Stacy is my fairy godmother, Alycia Tornetta is my magical muse. During the plotting of this book, she gave me advice. Her lessons on GMC (goal, motivation, conflict) have changed how I write. And her eagle eye and wordsmith skills kept me from embarrassing myself many times in this book. Girls, it's an honor working with you…but an even bigger one to call you my friends.

To our captain, Liz Pelletier, thank you for always keeping it real, for making me laugh, and for having such a teacher's spirit. My fabulous agent, Pam van Hylckama Vlieg, thanks for loving this story and believing in it as much as I do. I look forward to many, many, *many* years working together!

My mother-in-law Peggy was my instant form of research whenever I got confused or needed a certain detail. She read this book in record time, and her response e-mail made me all kinds of giddy. She may tie with my daughters for being my biggest fan. Speaking of reading in record time, my dad read this book when we were on vacation together. I admit I blushed knowing he was in the next room reading the body paint scene, but it meant SO much to know he was doing it. My mom not only reads every book I write but has also started writing herself. Our talks on plot and our favorite books always make me smile. Both of them keep our Cajun ancestry alive and help me pass it on to my children even here in Texas, and their open door policy for babysitting when I need a quiet space to write has been a blessing more times than I can count. I love all of you!

And finally, to you, my lovely, awesome readers, and to my fabulous Flirt Squad. Your emails, tweets, and reviews make me teary-eyed, giddy, and doing humorous happy dances that keep my girls laughing. As a bookworm, I know how many choices are out there, and I feel truly honored and blessed that you have chosen to read my stories. I hope they entertain you, give you a warm fuzzy, and help you escape the chaotic world we live in. Y'all are made of awesome.

About the Author

Rachel Harris grew up in New Orleans, where she watched soap operas with her grandmother and stayed up late sneak reading her mama's favorite romance novels. Now a Cajun cowgirl living in Houston, she still stays up way too late reading her favorite romances, only now, she can do so openly. She firmly believes life's problems can be solved with a hot, powdered-sugar-coated beignet or a thick slice of king cake, and that screaming at strangers for cheap, plastic beads is acceptable behavior in certain situations.

When not typing furiously or flipping pages in an enthralling romance, she homeschools her two beautiful girls and watches reality television with her amazing husband. *Taste The Heat* is her adult romance debut. She's the author of *My Super Sweet Sixteenth Century* and *A Tale of Two Centuries*. She loves hearing from readers! Find her at www. RachelHarrisWrites.com.

41363770R00135